英語
改錯速遞 增訂版

Quick Solutions to
Common English Errors

Revised Edition

嚴維明　編著

商務印書館

英語改錯速遞 (增訂版)

Quick Solutions to Common English Errors (Revised Edition)

編　　著：嚴維明
責任編輯：黃家麗
封面設計：張　　毅
出　　版：商務印書館 (香港) 有限公司
　　　　　香港筲箕灣耀興道 3 號東滙廣場 8 樓
　　　　　http://www.commercialpress.com.hk
發　　行：香港聯合書刊物流有限公司
　　　　　香港新界大埔汀麗路 36 號中華商務印刷大廈 3 字樓
印　　刷：中華商務彩色印刷有限公司
　　　　　香港新界大埔汀麗路 36 號中華商務印刷大廈 14 字樓
版　　次：2015 年 1 月第 1 版第 2 次印刷
　　　　　© 2013 商務印書館 (香港) 有限公司
　　　　　ISBN 978 962 07 0362 1
　　　　　Printed in Hong Kong

Publisher's Note 出版說明

　　從遊戲小組（play groups）初次接觸英語，到中小學及大學畢業，許多人學英語十幾年，但對於曾學過的英語知識，印象模糊，似是而非。問題出在哪裏？極可能是方法不對。

　　方法正確，事半功倍。〈速遞英語系列〉的核心理念是"要訣在握，一擊即中"。市場上的英語學習書很多，有的言之過詳，抓不住重點；有的過於簡單，停留於低層次的重複，使學習者勞而無功。本系列剛好相反，一則精要，有助抓住最基本、最關鍵的要訣，化繁為簡；二則提高，從學到知識要點提升至掌握規律，舉一反三，不斷強化。

　　〈速遞英語系列〉精心設計學習要點，將英語主題和難點分門別類，扼要點出規律，使學習者觸類旁通，並通過做練習題自我測試，以達到"速學速用"的目的。

商務印書館編輯出版部

Introduction 前言

　　許多初學者因經常犯相同錯誤，覺得如何也進步不了，心裏沮喪，但犯錯其實是學英語的必經過程，只要能從錯誤中學習，就可以掌握正確的英語。

　　從三十多年的英語教學經驗積累上千條誤句，針對語法、句式、詞彙等，篩選出最典型的錯誤 141 條，目的是發現、歸納錯誤的類型，有助學英語事半功倍。

　　本書先列出一誤一正的例句誤句，分析錯在何處，再指出如何糾正，然後舉一反三，最後提供練習題及答案。例如，先列出誤句 I broke my glasses yesterday so I have to buy a new one. 的正確形式為 I broke my glasses yesterday so I have to buy a new pair.，說明出錯原因是誤用 one，因 glasses 本身無法計量，不能用 one 代指一副眼鏡，要用 pair。同時學到同類詞語如 spectacles 及 spanners，都不能以 one 取代。這樣環環相扣，有助達到一理通百理明。

嚴維明

Usage Note 使用說明

用一個提問帶出主題。 ——— **10.18** 表示委員會成員，用 the committee，動詞是複數嗎？

✗ The committee **is** arguing among **itself**.

列出誤句及正確句子。 ——— ✓ The committee **are** arguing among
例句下有中譯。 **themselves**.

委員會成員當中意見不一。

What's wrong?

解釋錯誤之處 ——— **committee** 在這裏指的是委員會成員
(committee members)，不是指這個組
織，所以成員之間才可以「意見不一」，主
動詞因此要用複數形式。

Grammar Rules

歸納舉一反三的語法規 實語從句還包括介詞賓語從句，它的語序與
則，並舉英漢對照實際 動詞賓語的語序相同。例如：
例子。

The accident took place near **where**
we **were** playing.
事故離我們玩耍處不遠發生。

Grammar Tips

提出簡短易記的語法貼 **either...or...** 的主謂一致越來越不嚴格。
士。 許多人常將兩個主語合在一起用作複數。

Learn More

延伸學習與相關知識。 如果 **neither...nor...** 用作主語，謂語動詞的單複
數形式亦應作同樣安排。例如：

Neither Mary **nor** I am able to convince him.
瑪麗和我都不能說服他。

Comparison

舉英漢對照例子比較異 與 **just** 有一詞之差的 **just now**，也是「剛
同。 剛」的意思，但表示剛發生過的動作，因此
常與過去式連用。例如：

I saw Mary just **now**.
我剛見過瑪麗。

形式多樣化的練習題供 ——— **Practice** 練習 3
自我測試。

3.2 填字遊戲

Contents 目錄

1. Nouns
名詞

1.1 表示 "雪糕" 、 "綠茶" 等用複數嗎？

✗ There <u>are</u> many <u>ices</u> on the ground.

✓ There <u>is</u> much <u>ice</u> on the ground.

地上有許多冰。

___

What's wrong?

ice 是不可數名詞，解作 "冰" 時沒有複數。又如：

There is plenty of cracked <u>ice</u> in the bucket.
桶裏有很多碎冰塊。

Most of the Antarctic is covered with a mantle of snow and <u>ice</u>.
南極洲大部分地區覆蓋着一層冰雪。

但是，ice 解作 "雪糕" 時，便可帶不定冠詞，表示 "一杯" 、 "一份" 、 "一客" 等，並有複數。

The boys are licking at <u>ices</u>.
男孩在舔吃雪糕。

I'd like <u>an ice</u>.
我要一客雪糕。

Learn More

類似詞語有 beer 、 coffee 、 tea 等。例如：

<u>Beer</u> is my favourite drink.
啤酒是我最愛喝的飲料。

I ordered <u>a beer</u>.
我要了一杯啤酒。

China is well-known for its green <u>tea</u>.
中國以產綠茶著稱。

Two <u>teas</u>, please.
請來兩杯茶。

1.2 以 -s 結尾的名詞，動詞都用複數嗎？

✗ The <u>news are</u> splendid indeed.

✓ The <u>news is</u> splendid indeed.

這消息真好。

What's wrong?

news 不是 new 的複數形式。它是獨立名詞，形似複數，實為單數，故動詞必須使用單數。又如：

Good <u>news keeps</u> coming in.
好消息不斷傳來。

Bad <u>news has</u> wings.
壞事傳千里。—— 諺語

Learn More

像 news 這類名詞主要包括以 -s 結尾的學科名稱，例如：physics、economics、mathematics、statistics、electronics、linguistics、optics、athletics、politics、statistics、phonetics 等。

<u>Genetics has</u> developed rapidly.
遺傳學發展很快。

> **Grammar Tips**
> 一則消息要説 **a piece of news**。

1.3 表示 "英國人"，在 English 之前可用 an 嗎？

✗ My friend is <u>an English</u>.

✓ My friend is <u>an Englishman</u>.

✓ My friend is <u>English</u>.

我朋友是個英國人。

What's wrong?

English 解作 "英國人" 必須與定冠詞 the 連用，即 the English，統稱英國人，相等於 English people。要表示一個英國人，必須用 Englishman / Englishwoman。可以說 My friend is English.，但句中的 English 是形容詞。

She thinks she speaks English better than <u>the English</u>. 她認為自己英語講得比英國人還要好。

Three Englishmen are drinking beer in the garden. 三個英國人在花園裏喝啤酒。

Learn More

Dutch、French、Irish 用法與 English 相同。

<u>The French</u> love drinking wine.
法國人愛喝葡萄酒。

I saw two <u>Frenchmen</u> in the park.
我在公園裏看到兩個法國人。

> **Grammar Tips**
>
> 以 **-ese** 結尾的專有名詞，單複數相同。
>
> <u>The Japanese</u> are good at tea ceremony.
> 日本人精於茶道。
>
> <u>Two Japanese</u> are working in our company.
> 有兩個日本人在我們公司工作。

1.4 police 之後可加 -s 嗎？

✗ Two <u>polices</u> appeared at the corner.

✓ Two <u>policemen</u> appeared at the corner.

拐角上來了兩名警察。

What's wrong?

police 是個集體名詞，指維持治安的 "警察" 組織，而 policeman 指該組織的成員，因此 "兩名警察" 不可說 two polices。比較：

Several hundred <u>police</u> are on the track of the criminal.

幾百名警察正在追捕犯人。

Do you think we need to call <u>the police</u>?

你認為我們有必要叫警察嗎？

<u>Three policemen</u> are reportedly killed in the gunfight.

據報導，有三名警察在槍戰中喪生。

He joined <u>the police</u> in 2001.

他於 2001 年加入警隊。

Grammar Tips

police 解作一個 "組織" 時，要和定冠詞 **the** 連用，動詞始終用複數：

<u>The police</u> are now investigating the case.

警方正在調查這宗案件。

<u>The police</u> were contacted immediately after the murder.

謀殺案發生後馬上通知了警方。

1.5 表示 "幾根頭髮"，hair 要加 -s 嗎?

✗ My father already has some gray <u>hair</u>.

✓ My father already has some gray <u>hairs</u>.
我父親已經有幾根白頭髮。

What's wrong?

hair 是個集體名詞，是頭上所有頭髮的總稱。説 "幾根頭髮"，hair 就變成具體化，成了可與數字連用的可數名詞。比較:

I'll have my <u>hair</u> cut. 我要理髮了。

He brushed his <u>hair</u> and went out.
他梳梳頭髮便出了門。

There is not a grey <u>hair</u> on my aunt's head.
姨媽頭上沒有一根白頭髮。

Grammar Rules

同一個名詞，用作集體名詞是不可數，具體化時變成可數，這類名詞還有 fish、skin、fruit 等。例如:

I like <u>fish</u> and chips for lunch.
我喜歡吃炸魚薯條當作午餐。

Carp and sardine are two different <u>fishes</u>.
鯉魚和沙丁魚是兩種不同的魚。

This cream is used to protect the <u>skin</u>.
這種乳霜用來保護皮膚。

It takes three <u>skins</u> to make a coat.
三張毛皮才能做一件大衣。

> **Grammar Tips**
> 自然白的頭髮不能説 **white hair**。

1.6 homework、schoolwork 有複數嗎？

✗ The teacher often assigns us a lot of <u>homeworks</u>.

✓ The teacher often assigns us a lot of <u>homework</u>.

老師給了我們很多功課。

What's wrong?

學生作業稱為 work，給學生回家做的是 homework，兩者還可統稱 schoolwork，都沒有複數形式。

The boy finished his <u>work</u> in class.

那男孩上課時做完了作業。

She usually does her <u>homework</u> before dinner.

她通常在晚飯前做功課。

Have you any <u>schoolwork</u> today?

你今天有課外作業嗎？

Learn More

work 泛指 "工作" 時指不可數名詞，含 work 的其他複合詞也無複數，如 housework、fieldwork、farmwork 等。

I have got loads of <u>work</u> to do today.

我今天有一大堆工作要做。

My mother is busy with <u>housework</u>.

我媽媽忙於做家務。

> **Grammar Tips**
> **work** 的複數 **works** 解作 "作品"、"著作"、"工廠"、"廠房"。

1.7 結尾為 -o 的名詞，加 -s 即變複數嗎？

✗ <u>Tomatos</u> have many seeds.

✓ <u>Tomatoes</u> have many seeds.

蕃茄的籽很多。

What's wrong?

tomato 以 -o 結尾，-o 之前是個輔音字母，故複數形式要加 -es。

> The three big <u>tomatoes</u> weigh a pound.
> 三個大蕃茄重一磅。

> The boy picked <u>a tomato</u> in the garden.
> 那男孩在菜園裏摘了一個蕃茄。

Grammar Rules

potato、hero、mosquito、volcano 等名詞與 tomato 的情況相同，複數形式都需加 -es。但 -o 之前是元音字母的詞語，如 zoo、radio、bamboo、studio，以及一些縮略詞，如 photo(graph)、kilo(gramme)、memo(randum) 等，其複數形式只加 -s。另外，有些以 -o 結尾的名詞，複數可加 -s 或 -es，如 buffalo、cargo、tornado、volcano。

> He killed several <u>mosquitoes</u> before he went to bed.
> 他臨睡前打死了幾隻蚊。

> The city has two <u>zoos</u>.
> 這城市有兩個動物園。

> We took many <u>photos</u> in the park.
> 我們在公園裏拍了很多照片。

1.8 look、letter、custom 加 -s 有新含義嗎？

✗ The girl has a good look.

✓ The girl has good looks.

那女孩長得很漂亮。

What's wrong?

look 是"外表"、"神色"，沒有"漂亮"、"美貌"的意思，加 -s 之後 looks 含義不同。

She wears a confident look on her face.
她臉上帶着自信的神色。

Looks and youth are precious things in life.
美麗和年輕是人生寶貴的東西。

Comparison

custom、cloth、letter、manner、glass、good 等名詞，加 -s 之後也含義不同。比較下面兩組例句：

We must respect this local custom.
我們必須尊重這種當地風俗。

How long did it take you to pass the customs?
你過海關花了多長時間？

John is writing a letter to his mother.
約翰正在給媽媽寫信。

He is a man of letters.
他是個文學家。

1.9 複數名詞之前可否直接用 a？

✗ His uncle gave him <u>a binoculars</u>.

✓ His uncle gave <u>a pair of binoculars</u>.

他叔叔給了他一副望遠鏡。

What's wrong?

望遠鏡由兩個筒組成，因此 binoculars 是複數名詞，不能直接與不定冠詞連用。一副望遠鏡要用 a pair of 表示。

Learn More

有些物品由兩部分構成，表示"一副"、"一把"、"一雙"。例如：

a pair of
- scissors　一把剪刀
- pincers　一支鉗
- glasses　一副眼鏡
- trousers　一條褲

> **Grammar Tips**
>
> binoculars、pincers、glasses、trousers 是複數名詞，在不與 a pair of 連用作主語的情況下，動詞用複數形式。但 a pair of pincers 是"二合一"的整體，動詞要用單數形式。

1.10 表示 "死物" 的所有格時，可用 's 嗎？

✗ The <u>room's windows</u> are wide open.

✓ The <u>windows of the room</u> are wide open.

房間的窗戶敞開着。

What's wrong?

無生命概念的名詞，其所有格在一般情況下不用 -'s，
而是通過 of 完成。

Learn More

<u>The roof of the house</u> has fallen in.
那棟房子的屋頂已經塌陷。

<u>Many branches of the tree</u> broke in the
thunderstorm.
許多樹枝在雷暴中折斷了。

<u>The result of the exam</u> is not satisfactory.
考試成績不令人滿意。

<u>The rules of French grammar</u> are quite
complicated.
法語的語法規則相當複雜。

> **Grammar Tips**
> **a day's work**、**two days' visit** 是例外情況。

1.11 表示 "兩人共同擁有"，會重複用 's 嗎？

✗ We all admire <u>John's and Mary's</u> new car.

✓ We all admire <u>John and Mary's</u> new car.

我們全都羨慕約翰和瑪麗的新車。

What's wrong?

兩人共同擁有的人或物，不可兩個都用所有格，只可在最貼近共同擁有的人或物的人名之後加 's。

Learn More

<u>Al and Mary's</u> aunt died last week.

阿爾和瑪麗的姨媽上星期去世了。

<u>Cliff and John's</u> company was burnt down in a fire.

克利夫和約翰的公司在一場火災裏遭焚燬。

<u>Mills and Kidd's</u> behaviour was offensive at the party.

威爾斯和基德在宴會上的行為惹人反感。

With <u>Annie, Jane and Susan's</u> help, I passed the exam.

在安妮、珍和蘇珊的幫助下，我考試及格了。

1.12 在複合名詞中 's 放哪個位置？

✗ My <u>father's-in-law</u> house stands near the motorway.

✓ My <u>father-in-law's</u> house stands near the motorway.

我岳父的房子在高速公路附近。

What's wrong?

複合名詞或詞組的所有格出現在末尾，而非複合名詞或詞組的中央。

Learn More

The <u>commander-in-chief's</u> office is located in a cave. 總司令的辦公室設在山洞裏。

The <u>secretary general's</u> wife attended the ceremony yesterday.

秘書長夫人昨天參加了儀式。

The <u>President elect's</u> speech was very encouraging.

當選總統的演說很鼓舞人心。

Grammar Tips
複合名詞或詞組的複數變化規則與所有格不同，**-s** 加在中心詞詞尾，例如：**comrades-in-arms**（戰友）、**consuls general**（總領事）、**secretaries general**（秘書長）等。

Practice 練習 1

1.1 改正錯誤。

1. Physics are an interesting subject.

   _____

2. A cat has nine lifes.

   _____

3. The book is covered with dusts.

   _____

4. I have lots of schoolworks to do this evening.

   _____

5. The tree's lower branches almost touch the ground.

   _____

6. Twelve polices are working on that case.

   _____

7. Two Dutches sailed to Japan this morning.

   _____

8. This pair of shoes are not on sale.

   _____

1.2 改正錯誤。

1. You need to tidy up your hairs.

   _____

2. The government is recruiting responsible young adults to become policeman and woman.

   _____

3. That woman at the informations desk can answer all of our question.

   _____

4. To drink, all I want is glass of water.

   _____

5. For our project we are doing some researches on how plants suck water up into their leaves.

   _____

6. The school's secretary's briefcase was found under a bench.

   _____

7. I don't know what's wrong. I feel tired all the time.

   _____

8. That bunch of banana in the bowl looks very pretty.

   _____

9. Hundreds of containers hold all kinds of cargos at the Kwai Chung terminal.

   _____

10. There are three different kinds of bamboos in the garden.

   _____

2. Articles
冠詞

2.1 school、hospital 之前該用 the 嗎?

✗ The little girl goes to <u>the school</u> everyday.

✓ The little girl goes to <u>school</u> everyday.

那小女孩每天上學。

What's wrong?

school 解作"上學"、"讀書"時不帶冠詞,指具體某間學校時必須帶冠詞,又如:

My son began <u>school</u> at the age of 6.
我兒子六歲開始上學。

This child is not old enough for <u>school</u>.
這孩子還年幼,未夠年齡入學讀書。

Many foreign friends visited <u>the school</u> that day.
那天許多外籍朋友探訪那間學校。

<u>The school</u> is well-known in this region.
這間學校在本區很著名。

Usage

church、prison、court、hospital 與 school 用法相同,看以下兩組例子:

The criminal was thrown to <u>prison</u>.
罪犯給關進牢獄。

I have never seen <u>a prison</u> before.
我以前從未見過一所監獄。

The family go to <u>church</u> every week.
這家人每週都去教會崇拜。

<u>The church</u> stands at the foot of the hill.
那教堂聳立在山腳下。

2.2 概指某類事物該用 the 嗎？

✗ <u>The children</u> like to watch monkeys play in the zoo.

✓ <u>Children</u> like to watch monkeys play in the zoo.

孩子們喜歡去動物園看猴子嬉戲。

What's wrong?

孩子愛看猴子，是一般概念。這裏的 "孩子" 是指一類人，不是指某些特定的孩子，也不是指所有孩子，因此根據 "複數表示類別" 的原則不用定冠詞。

Learn More

Dictionaries are useful tools for learning a language.
詞典是學語言的有用工具。

Doctors earn more than other professionals.
醫生賺錢比其他專業人士多。

Balloons are often used for decoration.
氣球常用於裝飾。

Only mathematicians can solve this equation.
只有數學家才能解答這個方程式。

2.3 名詞用於句子第一部分時該用 the 嗎？

✗ <u>A pen</u> in hand, he is writing a letter to his girlfriend.

✓ <u>Pen</u> in hand, he is writing a letter to his girlfriend.

他手拿着筆正在寫信給女友。

What's wrong?

句子的第一部分在語法上稱為"獨立主格"。獨立主格的邏輯主語，即句中的 pen，無論是單數或複數，都不用冠詞。

Learn More

The policeman patrolled the area, <u>club</u> in hand.
警察拿着警棍在這地區巡邏。

<u>Books</u> in hand, the students went to the library.
學生們拿着書去圖書館。

<u>Bucket</u> in hand, Tom walked to the stream.
湯姆拿着水桶走到溪邊。

2.4 表示 "年代" 要用 the 嗎？

✗ Many terrorist attacks happened <u>in 1990's</u>.

✓ Many terrorist attacks happened <u>in the 1990's</u>.

1990 年代發生了許多恐怖主義襲擊事件。

What's wrong?

"1990 年代" 或 "20 世紀 90 年代" 有兩種表達形式，即 the 1990s 或 the 1990's，均讀作 the nineteen nineties。無論哪種，都不能缺少定冠詞。

Learn More

某年代 "初" 或 "末" 可用 early 或 late 修飾。

The <u>late</u> 1980s saw great changes in the world.
1980 年代末世界發生了巨變。

She was born in the <u>early</u> 1970s.
她出生於 1970 年代初。

> **Grammar Tips**
> 表示某一特定年份時，如 **in 2002**，該年份之前不用 **the**。

2.5 表示 "早、午、晚餐" 要用 the 嗎?

✗ When do you usually have <u>a breakfast</u>?

✓ When do you usually have <u>breakfast</u>?

你通常甚麼時候吃早餐?

What's wrong?

breakfast 之前一般不加冠詞,例如:

I had bacon and egg for <u>breakfast</u>.
我早餐吃了煙肉和雞蛋。

My mother is at <u>breakfast</u>.
我媽媽正在吃早餐。

但如果指一頓特定早餐,就必須用冠詞。
This morning I had a rich <u>breakfast</u>.
今早我吃了一頓豐富的早餐。

Learn More

She declined to have <u>lunch</u> with me.
她拒絕跟我同進午餐。

What do you usually have for <u>supper</u>?
晚餐你通常吃甚麼?

The committee members had a working <u>dinner</u> yesterday.
委員們昨天吃了一頓工作晚餐。

2.6 兩個對應詞一起用，要加 the 嗎？

✗ They became <u>the husband and the wife</u> in 2001.

✓ They became <u>husband and wife</u> in 2001.

他們在 2001 年結為夫婦。

What's wrong?

在英語中，兩個對應詞連用可省略冠詞，husband and wife 正屬於這類。又如：

What's their relationship? They are <u>husband and wife</u>.

他們是甚麼關係？他們是夫婦。

Learn More

連用兩個對應詞在英語中十分常見，都可省略冠詞。例如：

men and women	男男女女
young and old	老老少少
boys and girls	男孩和女孩
rich and poor	富人和窮人
north and south	南北
east and west	東西
officers and men	官兵

2.7 表示 "彈奏樂器" 要用 the 嗎？

✗ His brother plays <u>guitar</u> beautifully.

✓ His brother plays <u>the guitar</u> beautifully.

他哥哥彈結他彈得很出色。

What's wrong?

彈奏任何樂器，樂器名稱之前都必須加定冠詞 the。

Learn More

The girl began learning to play <u>the piano</u> from four.

那女孩從 4 歲開始學彈鋼琴。

Can you play <u>the violin</u>?

你會拉小提琴嗎？

Grammar Tips

說來有趣，玩任何球類，球類名稱之前都不加定冠詞 **the**。例如：

Boys like to play <u>football</u>.

男孩子喜歡踢足球。

She is good at playing <u>tennis</u>.

她網球打得不錯。

2.8 表示 "數量"，在 number 之前用 a 或 the？

✗ <u>The large number</u> of boys and girls were present at the dance.

✓ <u>A large number</u> of boys and girls were present at the dance.

許多男孩和女孩出席了舞會。

What's wrong?

這兩句的分別只是一個冠詞。number 與定冠詞連用表示 "…的數量"，與不定冠詞連用構成 a number of (若干)、a large number of (許多) 等習慣表達方式。

We must reduce the <u>number</u> of accidents on the motorways. 我們必須降低高速公路的事故數量。

A large <u>number</u> of tourists visit the Great Wall every year. 每年大批遊客遊覽長城。

Comparison

amount、quantity、variety 與 number 用法相似。

What is the <u>amount</u> of my bill? 我賬單上一共多少錢？

John owes Mary a large <u>amount</u> of money.
約翰欠瑪麗一大筆錢。

> **Grammar Tips**
>
> **number** 用於可數名詞，**amount** 用於不可數名詞。
>
> I spent a large <u>amount</u> of time reading this book.
> 我花了大量時間讀這本書。
>
> I read a large <u>number</u> of books every year.
> 我每年都讀大量的書。

2.9 表示"獨一無二"要用 the 嗎？

✗ It was very dark until <u>moon</u> rose.

✓ It was very dark until <u>the moon</u> rose.

月亮升起以前天很黑。

What's wrong?

moon 是世界上獨一無二的東西，要加定冠詞。

<u>Man first set his foot on <u>the moon</u> in 1969.</u>
人類於 1969 年第一次登上月球。

<u>The moon</u> shines over the quiet village.
月亮照耀着那個寧靜的村莊。

Grammar Rules

天體等世界上獨一無二的事物，都要加定冠詞。

<u>The sun</u> is down.
太陽落山了。

<u>The Jupiter</u> is the largest planet in the solar system.
木星是太陽系中最大的行星。

> **Grammar Tips**
>
> 如果 **sun**、**moon**、**sky** 之前有描繪性的定語，有時也可加不定冠詞。
>
> <u>A pale moon</u> hung low in the sky.
> 暗淡無光的月亮垂掛在天空。

2.10 以輔音字母 h 開頭的字該用 a 嗎？

✗ Jack is a honest farmer.

✓ Jack is an honest farmer.

傑克是個誠實的農夫。

What's wrong?

雖然 honest 以輔音字母 h 開頭，但 h 不發音。它的發音以元音 /ɒ/ 開頭。元音之前的不定冠詞要用 an。同樣 h 開頭的 house 卻說 a house。

Grammar Rules

正確使用 a 還是 an，不但要看後面名詞、形容詞等的拼寫，還要看其發音。European、university、one、uniform、UN 等貌似元音開頭，卻用 a。例如：

They are planning to set up a university.
他們計劃建立一所大學。

Yours is only a one-sided view.
你的只是一個片面看法。

> **Grammar Tips**
>
> **FBI、MP** 等貌似輔音開頭，卻用 **an**。例如：
>
> An FBI man discovered the secret.
> 一名聯邦調查人員發現了那個秘密。

2.11 表示"職務"要用 the 嗎？

✗ John was elected <u>the chairman</u> of the board of directors at the meeting.

✓ John was elected <u>chairman</u> of the board of directors at the meeting.

約翰在會上當選為董事局主席。

What's wrong?

be elected 指當選某範圍唯一的一個職務，那職務的名詞不用冠詞。又如：

He was elected <u>President</u> of the United States last fall.

他去年秋天當選美國總統。

Grammar Rules

名詞表示職務或頭銜，在句中用作表語、同位語、補語，一般不用冠詞。例如：

The General Assembly appointed him <u>Secretary General</u> of the United Nations.

聯合國大會任命他為聯合國秘書長。

George is <u>captain</u> of the football team.

喬治是足球隊隊長。

Mr. Smith, <u>former director</u> of the bureau, is to address the meeting.

前局長史密斯先生將在會上發表講話。

2.12 表示 "乘坐某種交通工具" 該用 the 嗎?

✗ Are you going there <u>by the train or by the plane</u>?

✓ Are you going there <u>by train or by plane</u>?
你去那裏乘火車還是飛機?

What's wrong?

含 by 的介詞短語表示交通工具時,中心詞不加冠詞。

She likes to travel <u>by sea / land / air</u>.
她喜歡乘船 / 車 / 飛機旅行。

He goes to work <u>by bus / car / tube /boat</u>.
他乘公共汽車 / 汽車 / 地鐵 / 船上班。

Grammar Rules

含 by 的介詞短語表示通訊途徑或生產方法,中心詞不加冠詞。例如:

He told me the news <u>by e-mail</u>.
他通過電郵告訴我這個消息。

Let's stay in touch <u>by telephone</u>.
讓我們保持電話聯繫吧。

The parcel was delivered <u>by hand</u>.
這包裏由專人親手送達。

Practice 練習 2

2.1 改正錯誤。

1. My mother bought a electric iron yesterday.

   _____

2. This table is made of the oak.

   _____

3. Jack left the school at the age of 17.

   _____

4. Some people go to the church and some don't.

   _____

5. The man has taken his first step into the space.

   _____

6. If the winter comes, can the spring be far behind?

   _____

7. The wounded were immediately taken to hospital nearby.

   _____

8. My brother showed me how to fly the kite.

   _____

2.2 用 a、an、the 或 Ø [無需用冠詞] 填空。

1. We might go to _____ Philippines or maybe to _____ Australia.

2. Can you see _____ Pacific Ocean from _____ Ocean Park?

3. I plan to go to _____ university in Hong Kong when I leave _____ school.

4. _____ umbrella is essential in _____ rainy season.

5. _____ moonlight is _____ sunlight reflected from _____ surface of _____ moon.

6. I had _____ soup and _____ sandwich for _____ lunch and _____ fruit for _____ dessert.

7. _____ bird in _____ hand is worth two in _____ bush.

8. I don't know how old my grandfather is. He was born in _____ 1950s.

9. My specialty in track and field events is _____ long jump.

10. The school put up _____ net so now we can play _____ volleyball or _____ badminton.

3. Pronouns
代詞

3.1 表示 "某人和我"，用 I 或 me？

✗ Mary invited only two classmates, <u>Jane and I</u>, to her picnic.

✓ Mary invited only two classmates, <u>Jane and me</u>, to her picnic.

瑪麗只邀請了兩個同學、珍和我跟她去野餐。

What's wrong?

Jane 和 I 是 two classmates 的同位語，two classmates 處於賓格位置，故 Jane 和 I 也必須使用賓格。I 的賓格是 me。

> On Christmas Day, Aunt Lena gave my sister a pen and her favourite nephew, <u>me</u>, a new bike!
> 聖誕節那天，莉娜姨媽給我妹妹一支筆，而給她最心愛的外甥，我，一輛新自行車！

Grammar Rules

代詞有主格、賓格、所有格之分，使用之前先要弄清楚代詞的語法地位。

> His elder sister is slightly taller than <u>he</u>.
> 他姐姐比他略高。

> My father walked between my mother and <u>me</u>.
> 我爸爸走在我媽媽和我中間。

> This book is <u>his</u>.
> 這本書是他的。

3.2 表示 "某人身體一部分"，該用 the 或 his / her？

✗ Mary <u>turned the head</u> to look at John.

✓ Mary <u>turned her head</u> to look at John.

瑪麗回過頭看約翰。

What's wrong?

在英語裏，表示某人身體的一部分時，那名詞之前要加物主代詞，這是中英文的不同，在中文裏，物主代詞會被省略，如上句不說 "瑪麗回過她的頭看約翰。"。又如：

She <u>kicked</u> the door <u>with her foot</u>.
她用腳踢門。

The little boy <u>brushes his teeth</u> every day.
小男孩每天刷牙。

Please <u>wash your hands</u> before a meal.
餐前請洗手。

> **Grammar Tips**
> 若強調是這個而不是那個部位，該名詞前可用定冠詞 **the** 代替物主代詞。如：
> The policeman <u>grasped</u> the thief <u>by the wrist</u>. 警察抓住小偷的手腕。
> He <u>hit</u> me <u>in the face</u>. 他擊中我的臉。

3.3 表示"我一個老朋友",用 an old friend of me 還是 mine?

✗ John is <u>an old friend of me</u>.

✓ John is <u>an old friend of mine</u>.

約翰是我的一個老朋友。

What's wrong?

me 是代詞 I 的賓格,不適用於本句。這句需要的是 I 的名詞性物主代詞 mine (my friends),表示所屬。

This isn't my bike. <u>Mine</u> is being repaired.
這不是我的自行車。我自己的那輛正在修理。

If your computer goes wrong, you can use <u>mine</u>.
要是你的電腦出了毛病,你可以用我的。

Learn More

we、you、he、she、they 的名詞性物主代詞分別是 ours、yours、his、hers、theirs,用法與 mine 相同。

This classroom is <u>ours</u>; that one is <u>theirs</u>.
這個課室是我們的;那個才是他們的。

My mother and <u>hers</u> are good friends.
我母親和她母親是好朋友。

3.4 表示某類人，可用人稱代詞 they 嗎？

✗ <u>They</u> who need the dictionary should sign here.

✓ <u>Those</u> who need the dictionary should sign here.

需要這本詞典的人在這裏簽名。

What's wrong?

表示某類人或物的定語從句中，不用人稱代詞 (如誤句中的 they) 充當關係代詞 (如誤句中的 who) 的先行詞，要用指示代詞 (如正句中的 those)。

He is among <u>those</u> who can speak English.
他是會講英語的人之一。

<u>Those</u> who choose may taste it.
想嚐的人可以嚐一下。

For <u>those</u> who are interested in music, the college offers a good program.
對那些對音樂感興趣的人，學院提供了一個很好的計劃。

Learn More

those 的單數 that 也可用於類似場合。例如：

What's <u>that</u> (which) you've got in your pocket?
你口袋裏放了甚麼？

<u>That</u> moving in the sky is a satellite.
在空中移動的是一個人造衛星。

3.5 否定兩個選擇可用 none 嗎？

✗ Jack has written two novels but <u>none</u> of them is successful.

✓ Jack has written two novels but <u>neither</u> of them is successful.

傑克寫了兩本小說，沒有一本成功。

What's wrong?

否定三者或以上用 none，否定兩者應該用 neither。比較下列兩組例句：

She gave me several ballpoints, but I like <u>none</u> of them.

她給我幾支圓珠筆，但我一支都不喜歡。

She gave me two ballpoints, but I like <u>neither</u> of them.

她給我兩支圓珠筆，但我一支都不喜歡。

<u>None</u> of his colleagues knows where he has gone.

他的同事都不知道他去了哪裏。

<u>Neither</u> of his two sisters knows where he has gone.

他的兩個妹妹都不知道他去了哪裏。

Comparison

none 和 neither 的反義詞是 anyone 和 either。比較：

Gentlemen, can <u>anyone</u> of you help that lady?

先生們，你們誰能幫一下那位女士？

You two gentlemen, can <u>either</u> of you go and help that lady?

你們兩位先生，誰能去幫一下那位女士？

3.6 如何正確使用 that 和 which？

✗ The computer, <u>that</u> has become very useful in daily life, is owned by many homes in China.

✓ The computer, <u>which</u> has become very useful in daily life, is owned by many homes in China.

電腦在日常生活中很有用，中國許多家庭都有了。

What's wrong?

... that has become very useful in daily life 是非限制性定語從句，表示物的關係代詞用 which，不用 that。

> The village has 35 houses, more than one-third of <u>which</u> are newly built.
> 村裏有 35 棟房子，其中三分之一以上是新蓋的。
>
> These peach trees, <u>which</u> I planted five years ago, bear much fruit every year.
> 這幾棵桃樹是我五年前種的，現在每年都結很多桃子。

Grammar Rules

在非限制性定語從句中，表示人的關係代詞要用 who 或 whom，也不能用 that，而在限制性定語從句中是可以的。

> The community had 230 men, many of <u>whom</u> went to the front during the war.
> 這個社區有 230 名男子，其中許多在戰時去了前線。
>
> Dr. William, <u>who</u> is a good friend of mine, has saved many lives.
> 威廉醫生是我的一個好朋友，他已挽救多人的生命。

3.7 表示"一副眼鏡、一把剪刀"，用 one 還是 pair？

✗ I broke my glasses yesterday so I have to buy a new <u>one</u>.

✓ I broke my glasses yesterday so I have to buy a new <u>pair</u>.

我昨天摔破了眼鏡，因此我不得不買一副新的。

What's wrong?

one 常用於代替上文中的可數名詞或可數名詞短語，但 glasses 是一種特殊情況，雖然是複數形式，但必須通過 pair 才可表示複數，所以 one 不可指"一副眼鏡"。注意下列例子中的用法：

> This skirt is a bit small. I need a bigger <u>one</u>.
> 這條裙子小了一點，我要一條大點的。

> These photos are fine <u>ones</u>.
> 這些照片拍得不錯。

Learn More

trousers、spectacles、spanners、scissors 也同樣不能用 one 取代。例如：

> Your pajamas have worn in several places. You can wear my <u>pair</u> / mine.
> 你的睡衣褲有幾處磨破了。你可以穿我那套。

> Bring your scissors. An old <u>pair</u> will do.
> 帶上你的剪刀，舊的就行。

3.8 表示 "不少"，可説 quite few 嗎？

✗ <u>Quite few</u> students failed in the examination.

✓ <u>Quite a few</u> students failed in the examination.

不少學生考試不及格。

What's wrong?

表示否定，意思是 "很少"、"幾乎沒有"；而表示肯定，意思是 "幾個"，因此 "不少" 不能説 quite few。比較下列例子：

There were <u>few</u> cars in the streets at that hour.
那個時間街上汽車很少。
The small town has only <u>a few</u> cars.
小鎮只有幾輛汽車。
<u>Few</u> people want to buy this.
幾乎沒有人會買這種東西。
I have <u>a few</u> things to tell you.
我有幾件事要告訴你。

Grammar Rules

few 用於可數名詞之前，不可數名詞之前用 little，含義相同。

Susan has <u>little</u> money. 蘇珊幾乎一點錢也沒有。
I like <u>a little</u> milk in my tea. 我喝茶喜歡放一點牛奶。

3.9 只用 enjoy 可表示 "玩得高興" 嗎？

✗ Did you <u>enjoy</u> at the seaside?

✓ Did you <u>enjoy yourselves</u> at the seaside?

你們在海邊玩得快活嗎？

What's wrong?

enjoy 是及物動詞，必須有賓語；解作 "玩得快樂" 時，它的賓語是反身代詞。

> Did she <u>enjoy herself</u> at the party last night?
> 她在昨晚的派對上玩得開心嗎？

> I <u>enjoyed myself</u> during the summer vacation.
> 我暑假過得很快活。

Learn More

常以反身代詞作賓語的動詞有 avail、express、offer、pride。

> I cannot <u>express myself</u> clearly in English.
> 我不會用英語清楚表達自己。

> Grasp it when opportunity <u>offers</u> itself.
> 機會來了就要抓住。

> Mary <u>prides herself</u> on her ability to speak English fluently.
> 瑪麗為自己能説一口流利英文感到自豪。

3.10 表示 "所屬"，可用 which 嗎？

✗ SOI is a non-governmental organization <u>which</u> sole purpose is to help mentally retarded children.

✓ SOI is a non-governmental organization <u>whose</u> sole purpose is to help mentally retarded children.

✓ SOI is a non-governmental organization, the sole purpose <u>of which</u> is to help mentally retarded children.

國際特奧會是個非政府組織，它的唯一宗旨是幫助弱智兒童。

What's wrong?

which 僅是關係代詞，沒有所屬的意思。因此，在上述從句中要用 which 的所有格 whose (= of which)。

There are several words in this article, <u>whose</u> meanings (the meanings of which) I don't understand. 這篇文章裏有幾個詞的意思我不明白。
Nobody wants the house <u>whose</u> roof has fallen in. 沒人會要這屋頂已塌陷的房子。

Grammar Rules

who 的所有格也是 whose (= of whom)，在從句中用作關係代詞：

He is an expert in this field, <u>whose</u> opinions we should listen to. 他是這行的專家，他的意見我們該聽。

Practice 練習 3

3.1 改正錯誤。

1. Are there anybody who would like to go swimming with me?

   _____

2. The baby cried for mother.

   _____

3. When John went to town, he bought some chocolate for his brother and him.

   _____

4. They who are interested in these magazines may borrow them.

   _____

5. It's impossible for Jack and I to finish their task before dark.

   _____

6. This umbrella is my; that one is her.

   _____

7. The ink is used up. I have to buy a new one.

   _____

8. None of us speak Russian very well.

   _____

3.2 填字遊戲

Across Down	a	b	c	d	e	f	g	h	i	j	k	l	m	n	o	p	q
1																	
2																	
3																	
4																	
5																	
6																	
7																	
8																	
9																	
10																	

橫

1 j This desk does not belong to our class so it must be _____.

2 f I can't decide _____ I like better.

2 o Albert said please return the book to _____, when you have finished with it.

3 n The principal spoke to my friend about _____.

4 j You can't have it, it's _____!

6 e _____ Ed nor Jack are to blame. They both say Paul did it.

9 a She said she would do it _____.

直

c 6 These trousers are too short. Do you have another _____?

e 6 _____ of these web sites has trustworthy information.

g 1 You saw Ms Wong holding hands with _____?

45

j 1 Their teacher offered to help but the students said they could do it _____.

m 1 _____ doesn't take long to do.

o 1 _____ is the girl I've been looking for.

4. Numbers
數詞

4.1 表示一段時間，動詞用單數嗎？

✗ <u>Twenty years</u> <u>are</u> a long time.

✓ <u>Twenty years</u> <u>is</u> a long time.

二十年是一段很長的時間。

What's wrong?

句中的 twenty years 是指一段時間，構成整體概念，因此動詞使用單數。比較下列例句：

<u>Ten years</u> / <u>two weeks</u> is just a wink.
十年 / 兩個星期時間只是一眨眼功夫。

<u>Ten years</u> have passed since we met last time.
自從我們上次見面以來，十年過去了。

<u>Two weeks</u> are allowed for making the necessary preparations.
獲准用兩週完成必須的準備工作。

Grammar Rules

不可數名詞之前如有具體數量，動詞常用複數形式。

100,000 square metres of housing <u>were</u> completed north of the town last year.
去年鎮北有 10 萬平方米的住房完工。

One million tons of iron ore <u>were</u> exported to that country.
向該國出口了一百萬噸鐵礦石。

4.2 表示數字，動詞用複數嗎？

✗ **29 minus 9 <u>make</u> 20.**

✓ **29 minus 9 <u>makes</u> 20.**

29 減 9 等於 20。

What's wrong?

29 是個數字，不是指某物具體數量，因此動詞用單數。

333 minus 333 <u>is</u> 0.

333 減 333 等於 0。

Grammar Rules

數學運算中，減法與除法的動詞 "等於" 用單數，乘法與加法的動詞單複數均可。例如：

What <u>is</u> / <u>are</u> 5 plus 12?

5 加 12 等於幾？

3 times 9 <u>is</u> / <u>are</u> 27.

3 乘 9 等於 27。

35 divided by 7 <u>is</u> 5.

35 除 7 等於 5。

4.3 metre 的複數形式受形容詞影響嗎？

✗ This river is 20 <u>metre</u> <u>wide</u>.

✓ This river is 20 <u>metres</u> <u>wide</u>.

這條河 20 米寬。

What's wrong?

metre 的複數形式不受後面形容詞的影響，仍需加 -s。"數量 + 形容詞" 的公式可表示物體的長、寬、高、深、年齡等。

> She'<u>s</u> 50 years old but doesn't look her age.
>
> 她 50 歲，但看不出她年紀那麼大。
>
> The television tower <u>is</u> 120 metres tall.
>
> 這電視塔高 120 米。

Grammar Rules

"數量 + 形容詞" 用作定語，要用連字符 (-) 相連，量詞不用複數。例如：

> This 13-<u>year</u>-old boy is already a university student.
>
> 這 13 歲的男孩子已是個大學生。
>
> Do you know there is a 20-<u>metre</u>-deep cave over there?
>
> 你知不知那邊有個 20 米深的山洞？

4.4 表示 "一次、兩次"，可用 one time、two times 嗎？

✗ Sylvia links the Internet <u>two times</u> a day.

✓ Sylvia links the Internet <u>twice</u> a day.

西爾維婭一天上網兩次。

What's wrong?

在英語中，"一次" 及 "兩次" 有專門的詞，是 once 及 twice，不說 one time 或 two times。

I practise English <u>once</u> a day.
我每天練習英語一次。

Mary visits her aunt <u>twice</u> a month.
瑪麗每月探望她姨媽兩次。

Grammar Rules

很少用專門副詞 thrice 表示 "三次"，常用 three times 表示 "三次"。"四次" 或以上也用 times 表示。例如：

She knocked <u>three times</u> / <u>thrice</u> at the door.
她敲了門三次。

在英文口語中，也會用 a hundred times 表示 "多次"。

I've told you <u>a hundred times</u>.
我已向你說過多次。

4.5 如何用 thousand 表示 "成千上萬" ？

✗ There are more than fifty <u>thousands</u> books in our library.

✓ There are more than fifty <u>thousand</u> books in our library.

我們圖書館有五萬多冊藏書。

What's wrong?

thousand 用作確實數字修飾名詞時不可有複數，只在表示 "成千上萬"、"許許多多" 的籠統概念時才可加 -s，並常跟 of 連用。

Two <u>thousand</u> and five delegates attended the conference today.
二千零五個代表出席了今天的會議。

<u>Thousands of</u> refugees flooded that country.
成千上萬難民湧入那國家。

Learn More

與 thousand 用法相同的數字有 ten、hundred、million、billion。

The auditorium in our school can seat five <u>hundred</u> people.
我們學校禮堂可坐 500 人。

There are <u>hundreds of</u> newspapers and magazines in our reading-room.
我們閱覽室有幾百種報章雜誌。

China has a population of 130 <u>million</u> people.
中國有 13 億人口。

<u>Millions of</u> people lost their homes in the war.
幾百萬人在戰爭裏失去家園。

4.6 表示 "兩天遊覽"，是在 day 之後加 -s 嗎？

✗ After <u>two day</u> visit, we know much about this city.

✓ After <u>two days</u>' visit, we know much about this city.

✓ After <u>a two-day</u> visit, we know much about this city.

兩天遊覽後，我們對這城市有許多了解。

What's wrong?

"兩天遊覽" 不能說 two day visit。這個意思可用兩種結構表達：

1) two days' visit； 2) a two-day visit。又如：

During my <u>10-day</u> stay in Paris, I visited the Eiffel Tower.
留在巴黎的 10 天內，我參觀了埃菲爾鐵塔。
During <u>10 days</u>' stay in Paris, I visited the Eiffel Tower.
留在巴黎的 10 天內，我參觀了埃菲爾鐵塔。

Grammar Rules

第一種結構可歸納為 "數字 + 量詞 (如複數的話留 -s) + 所有格符號 (') + 名詞"； 第二種結構可歸納為 "數字 + 量詞 (如複數的話去 -s) + 連字符 (-) + 名詞"。第二種結構之前要冠詞。例如：

The <u>twelve-hour</u> flight almost exhausted me.
十二個小時的飛行使我幾乎筋疲力盡。

Through <u>three years</u>' training, he became a real professional.
通過三年培訓，他成為真正的專業人士。

4.7 如何用 dozen 表示"十幾個"？

✗ My mother bought <u>two dozens</u> oranges yesterday.

✓ My mother bought <u>two dozen</u> oranges yesterday.

我媽媽昨天買了兩打橙。

What's wrong?

dozen 表示確實的數量概念"十二個"，即"一打"，也可表示大致的數量概念"十幾個"。前者不能有複數，後者可加 -s，並常和 of 連用，即 dozens of。

> My mother bought one and a half dozen eggs in the market.
> 我媽媽在市場上買了一打半雞蛋。
> I've <u>dozens of</u> problems to deal with.
> 我要處理的問題很多。

Grammar Rules

與 dozen 同類的還有 score（二十個）等。但 score 表示確實數量要和 of 連用，不直接用作定語，這時是單複數同形。表示大致數量和 dozen 相同，複數要加 -s。例如：

> <u>Two scores of</u> people were present at the inauguration ceremony.
> 四十人出席了開幕典禮。
> I've <u>scores of</u> problems to deal with.
> 我要處理許多問題。

4.8 表示"世界大戰"，用 World War I 還是 the world war I？

✗ **The World War I** broke out in 1914.

✓ **World War I** broke out in 1914.

✓ **The First World War** broke out in 1914.

✓ **World War One** broke out in 1914.

第一次世界大戰於 1914 年爆發。

What's wrong?

世界大戰有三種表達形式，分別是 World War I、The First World War broke out in 1914.、World War One broke out in 1914.。第二次世界大戰是 World War II (讀 作 World War Two)、the Second World War、World War Two，三者不能混淆。

Grammar Rules

表示次序的三種形式可歸納為：1) 名詞 + 羅馬數字 / 阿拉伯數字；2) 定冠詞 + 序數詞 + 名詞；3) 名詞 + 英語數字。例如：

This is Volume III / Volume Three / the Third Volume of *The Complete Works of Shakespeare*.
這是《莎士比亞全集》第三卷。

Let's turn to the Lesson 20 / 20th Lesson.

讓我們翻到第 20 課。

4.9 表示 "增加兩倍"，可用 twice 嗎？

✗ Our output this year is <u>twice</u> as big as last year.

✓ Our output this year is <u>three times</u> as big as last year.

我們今年產量比去年增加兩倍。

What's wrong?

twice as big as 的意思是 "兩倍那麼大"，實際上只增加一倍。因此，只有將英語中的數字增加 1 才能與中文一致。

This room is <u>twice as large as</u> that one.
這房間是那房間的兩倍大 / 這房間比那房間大一倍。

Our income is <u>three times as much as</u> theirs.
我們的收入是他們的三倍 / 我們的收入比他們多兩倍。

Learn More

同一事物的倍數較常使用動詞 double、treble。例如：

Our output <u>has doubled</u> this year.
我們今年產量增加了一倍 / 我們今年產量是去年的兩倍。

His income <u>has trebled</u> during the last three years.
他的收入在過去三年內增加了兩倍 / 他的收入是三年前的三倍。

Practice 練習 4

4.1 改正錯誤。

1. We have six fifty-minutes classes every day.
   _____

2. 81 divided by 9 make 9.
   _____

3. Many important battles took place during the World
   War II.
   _____

4. My mother bought some two-dollars-a-kilo fish.
   _____

5. More than two hundreds students attended the
   lecture.
   _____

6. She bought two dozens of eggs in the supermarket.
   _____

7. The twelve years old girl is my sister.
   _____

8. The pagoda must be 50-metre tall.
   _____

4.2 選出正確答案。

1. We live on the eight / eighth floor.

2. How many time / times do I have to tell you – turn
   off the lights when you leave the room!

3. George won the race in the 11-13 year old/olds
   category.

4. How <u>many / much</u> money do you need to save to buy that computer?

5. The population of Hong Kong has grown to over seven <u>million / millions</u> people.

6. Take these tablets twice a <u>day / days</u> for one week.

7. Add 1 <u>cup / cups</u> of water and heat to 110 <u>degree / degrees</u>.

8. Look at all those birds! There must be dozen / dozens and <u>dozen / dozens</u> of them.

9. There are 8 different <u>title / titles</u> in the Harry Potter series. The <u>book / Book</u> two is my favourite.

4.3 用英文表達時間。

1. If this is August, last month was _____.

2. It's now November. In three months it will be _____.

3. I was born in 2003. My elder brother is four years older than me. He was born in _____.

5. Verbs
動詞

5.1 表示"實際存在的可能"，可用 can 嗎？

✗ I'm afraid it <u>can</u> rain tomorrow.

✓ I'm afraid it <u>might</u> rain tomorrow.

✓ I'm afraid it <u>may</u> rain tomorrow.

我擔心明天可能要下雨。

What's wrong?

"明天可能要下雨"是實際有可能發生，因此不能用 can，要用 may 或 might。can 表示有可能偶然發生，常與適當的時間、頻率狀語連用。比較下列兩組例句：

He <u>can</u> be angry at times.
他有時會發脾氣。

He <u>may</u> be angry at this.
他一見這個會生氣。

The lake <u>can</u> freeze, even in late autumn.
即使在深秋湖面也會結冰。

The lake <u>may</u> freeze tomorrow.
明天湖面可能會結冰。

5.2 dare 何時用作動詞，何時用作助動詞？

✗ She <u>dare</u> not to walk alone at night.

✓ She <u>dare</u> not walk alone at night.

✓ She <u>does not dare</u> to walk alone at night.

晚上她不敢獨自一個人走。

What's wrong?

像 dare 這個情態動詞，有兩種用法。一種用作助動詞，例如：

He <u>dare</u> not speak to me.
他不敢跟我講話。

<u>Dare</u> you look down the cliff?
你敢從懸崖往下看嗎？

I <u>dare</u> say he is the cleverest boy in our class.
我敢說，他是我們班上最聰明的男孩子。

一種用作實義動詞，例如：

He <u>does not dare</u> (to) go there.
他不敢去那裏。

Does anyone <u>dare</u> (to) swim across the river?
有人敢游過河嗎？

How <u>did she dare</u> (to) say that!
她怎敢說那種話！

Grammar Tips
後一種形式常用於疑問句或否定句。

5.3 表示 "要被修理"，用 to repair 或 to be repaired？

✗ His watch **needs to repair**.

✓ His watch **needs to be repaired**.

✓ His watch **needs repairing**.

他的手錶需要修一修。

What's wrong?

在此句中，his watch 處於主語位置，是 "被修理"，因此用作賓語的動詞不定式要用被動語態。更常見的是用動名詞作 need 的賓語。

> Your shirt **needs washing / to be washed**.
> 你的襯衣要洗一洗了。
>
> The old house **needs renovating / to be renovated**.
> 這老房子要翻新一下了。

Comparison

need 和 dare 用法共同之處，是兩者都有兩種表達形式，可用作助動詞或實義動詞，例如：

> **Need** I tell him the news? 我需要告訴他這消息嗎？
> Does he **need** to tell her the news?
> 他需要告訴她這消息嗎？

但 need 是真正的實義動詞，直接擁有賓語，例如：

> Do you **need** any help? 你需要幫忙嗎？
> He **needs** something to eat. 他需要一點吃的東西。

> **Grammar Tips**
> need 用作情態動詞時，主要用於疑問句或否定句。

5.4 表示 "停下來買"，stop 後接 buying 還是 to buy ？

✗ When my father came in, we <u>stopped to talk</u>.

✓ When my father came in, we <u>stopped talking</u>.

我爸爸進來時，我們都不講話了。

What's wrong?

用 stop 要特別注意：如後接動詞不定式，意思是停下來做另一件事；如後接動名詞，意思是停止做某事。比較下列兩組例句：

On my way home, I <u>stopped to buy</u> a magazine.
我在回家路上停下來買一本雜誌。

I <u>stopped reading</u> the magazine and looked up.
我停止看雜誌，抬起頭來。

We <u>stopped to have</u> a rest.
我們停下來休息一會。

We <u>stop working</u> at five.
我們五點鐘停止工作。

Comparison

pause 與 stop 用法相似。例如：

He <u>paused</u> before the mirror to adjust his tie.
他停在鏡前整理領帶。

5.5 to- 不定式中，主語和主句如何一致？

✗ **To start early, <u>everything</u> is ready.**

✓ **To start early, <u>we</u> have got everything ready.**

為了一大早出發，一切都準備好了。

What's wrong?

這句錯在 to start early 的邏輯主語與主句不一致。也就是說，在以動詞不定式作狀語時，其邏輯主語要和主句保持一致。例如：

> To show her hospitality, <u>the hostess</u> guided the guests on a tour of her house.
> 為要顯出她好客，女主人帶賓客參觀她的家。

> In order to serve the country well tomorrow, <u>we</u> must study hard today.
> 為了明天為國效力，我們今天必須努力學習。

> To prevent floods, <u>the farmers</u> have strengthened the dyke along the river.
> 為了防止洪水泛濫，農民已加固河堤。

5.6 表示 "被下令"，make 要後接 to 嗎？

✗ She <u>was</u> finally <u>made do</u> the work.

✓ She <u>was</u> finally <u>made to do</u> the work.

她最後只得做這事。

What's wrong?

動詞不定式用作 make 的賓語補語時，在主動語態中不帶 to，但在被動語態中 to 不可缺少。

The policeman <u>made</u> him stand against the wall.
那警察命令他靠牆站着。

→ He <u>was made to</u> stand against the wall.
他被下令靠牆站着。

They <u>made</u> her <u>see</u> the reason.
他們使她明白原因。

→ She <u>was made to</u> see the reason.
她被告知原因。

Grammar Rules

動詞不定式用作 help 的賓語補語時，在主動語態中可不帶 to，但在被動語態中 to 不可缺少。例如：

They <u>helped</u> me (<u>to</u>) review the lessons.
他們幫我複習功課。

→ I <u>was helped to</u> review the lessons.
我在別人幫助下複習功課。

5.7 現在分詞用作狀語，主語和主句如何一致？

✗ <u>While crossing the road</u>, my mobile phone rang.

✓ <u>While I was crossing the road</u>, my mobile phone rang.

過馬路時，我的手機響起。

What's wrong?

分詞用作狀語時，邏輯主語要和主句保持一致，誤句的 my mobile phone 不能充當 crossing the street 的邏輯主語。

> <u>Singing</u> merrily, <u>the little girl</u> went upstairs.
> 小女孩一邊快樂唱着歌，一邊走上樓。

> <u>Hearing</u> this, <u>she</u> became very worried.
> 聽到這情況，她心裏很擔心。

> <u>Having written</u> a letter, <u>he</u> mailed it on his way to work.
> 寫完信後，他上班時寄出了它。

5.8 表示"加熱", 在 heat 後加 -ing 還是 -ed?

✗ <u>Heating</u>, the metal expands.

✓ <u>Heated</u>, the metal expands.

金屬受熱膨脹。

What's wrong?

heat 是及物動詞, 是"加熱"的意思。金屬本身不會加熱, 因此用作狀語的應是過去分詞, 以便保持邏輯主語一致。又如:

<u>Shocked</u>, <u>he</u> stood motionless against the wall.
他大吃一驚, 靠在牆上一動也不動。

<u>Moved</u> by his offer, <u>Mary</u> was at a loss what to say.
瑪麗給他的提議打動, 不知道該講甚麼。

<u>Tom</u>, <u>accompanied</u> by his father, went to the airport.
湯姆在父親陪同下前往機場。

5.9 表示 "喜愛"，enjoy 後接不定式還是動名詞？

✗ Young girls <u>enjoy to kick</u> the shuttlecock.

✓ Young girls <u>enjoy kicking</u> the shuttlecock.

小女孩喜歡踢毽子。

What's wrong?

動詞 enjoy 表示 "喜愛"，不後接動詞不定式，而後接動名詞。

> She <u>enjoys</u> listening to music while working.
> 她喜歡一邊工作一邊聽音樂。

> Young boys <u>enjoy</u> playing football.
> 小男孩喜歡踢足球。

> Jack <u>enjoys</u> going fishing with his father.
> 傑克喜歡跟他爸爸釣魚。

Learn More

賓語不用動詞不定式而用動名詞的及物動詞很多，其中包括 avoid、deny、escape、finish、resume、risk 等。

> Betty has to <u>avoid</u> eating fatty food.
> 貝蒂不得不避免吃高脂食物。

> The thief <u>denied</u> having stolen her purse.
> 小偷否認偷了她的錢包。

> She <u>has resumed</u> writing the book.
> 她又提筆寫那本書。

5.10 表示 "剛剛"，just now 用於現在完成式嗎？

✗ Jane <u>just</u> <u>bought</u> a digital camera.

✓ Jane <u>has just bought</u> a digital camera.

珍剛買了一個數碼相機。

What's wrong?

在英式英語中，副詞 just 表示一個剛完成的動作，因此要與完成時連用。

> She <u>has just returned</u> from Washington.
> 她剛從華盛頓回來。

> My sister <u>has just been</u> to the supermarket.
> 我妹妹剛去過超級市場。

> My boss <u>had just left</u> for Tokyo when you arrived.
> 你到達時，我老闆剛出發去東京。

Comparison

與 just 有一詞之差的 just now，也是 "剛剛" 的意思，但表示剛發生過的動作，因此常與過去式連用。例如：

> I saw Mary <u>just now</u>.
> 我剛見過瑪麗。

> John came to visit us <u>just now</u>.
> 約翰剛來探望過我們

5.11 兩個動作發生時間不同，該如何用過去式、過去完成式？

✗ Before the movie <u>was</u> over, many <u>left</u> their seats for home.

✓ <u>Before</u> the movie <u>was</u> over, many <u>had left</u> for home.

電影放完之前，許多人已經起身回家了。

What's wrong?

在以 after、as soon as、before、until 等連詞連接的複合句中，如果兩個動作有明顯的時間差別或先後次序之分，先發生者常用過去完成式。"起身回家"顯然發生在"電影放完"之前，因此要用過去完成式。又如：

<u>After</u> she had worked in the circus for three years, she decided to give up the job.

她在馬戲團內做了三年後，決定放棄那份工作。

My father had lived in that old house for nearly 10 years <u>before</u> he moved to Los Angeles.

我爸爸搬到洛杉磯前，在那棟老房子裏住了近 10 年。

I hadn't realized that he wasn't Japanese <u>until</u> he spoke.

直到他開口講話，我才知道他原來不是日本人。

5.12 將來的動作會用過去式表達嗎?

✗ He <u>said</u> in his e-mail that he <u>is leaving</u> for Canada soon.

✓ He <u>said</u> in his e-mail that he <u>was leaving</u> for Canada soon.

✓ He <u>says</u> in his e-mail that he <u>is leaving</u> for Canada soon.

他在電郵裏說,很快他就要去加拿大。

What's wrong?

主句是過去式,賓語從句也要用過去式,即使描述的可能是將來的動作。

Jane <u>said</u> she <u>had been to</u> Canada twice.
珍說她去過加拿大兩次。

She <u>told</u> me that her father <u>would buy</u> her a computer.
她對我說,她爸爸將買部電腦給她。

My classmates <u>thought</u> that I <u>was making</u> progress.
同學們認為我正在進步。

> **Grammar Tips**
> 用賓語從句描述一個真理時,不論主句是甚麼時態,從句始終用現在式,例如:
> The teacher <u>told</u> the students that the earth <u>revolves</u> round the sun.
> 老師對學生們說,地球圍繞太陽轉動。

5.13 表示"過去不知道但現在知道"，該用 I don't know 嗎？

✗ <u>I don't know</u> that it is so hard to learn a foreign language.

✓ <u>I didn't know</u> that it was so hard to learn a foreign language.

我不知道學一門外語是那麼辛苦的。

What's wrong?

"我不知道"有兩種概念，一種是"過去不知道，但現在知道"，另一種是"現在不知道"，上句屬於前者，所以主句的動詞要用過去式。比較下列兩組例子：

> <u>I don't know</u> where she lives now.
> 我不知道她現在住在哪裏。
>
> <u>I didn't know</u> she was such a great swimmer.
> 我不知道她原來是個游泳高手。
>
> He <u>doesn't know</u> why the old woman is so sad.
> 他不知道那老太太為何那麼傷心。
>
> He <u>did not know</u> that the old woman suffered from cancer. 他不知道那老太太原來患了癌症。

Learn More

動詞 expect、imagine 等常出現這樣的時間差異。

> The burglar <u>did not expect</u> that he would be sentenced to ten years' imprisonment.
> 竊賊沒料到會被判十年徒刑。
>
> The situation is not as bad as we <u>imagined</u>.
> 形勢沒我們原先想像的那麼差。

5.14 表示"過去的過去"可用過去式嗎?

✗ She <u>was</u> angry because she found he <u>left</u> without saying good-bye.

✓ She <u>was</u> angry because she found he <u>had left</u> without saying good-bye.

她很生氣,因為她發現他沒說再見就走了。

What's wrong?

誤句的狀語從句在時態上沒有時間差異。"發現"在後,"走"在前,因此要用過去完成式。

> She later found out that he <u>had been lying</u> to her.
> 她後來發現他一直對她說謊。

> They arrived at the station only to find that the train <u>had left</u>.
> 他們抵達車站,結果發現火車已開走了。

Learn More

表現"過去的過去"是過去完成式的基本功能。又如:

> Will suddenly remembered that he <u>had not locked</u> the door.
> 威爾突然想起他沒鎖門。

> They <u>had moved</u> to Sydney three years before their father died.
> 父親死時他們已搬到悉尼三年。

5.15 if-從句可用將來式嗎？

✗ What shall we do <u>if it will rain tomorrow</u>?

✓ What shall we do <u>if it rains tomorrow</u>?

明天下雨我們做甚麼？

What's wrong?

在條件狀語從句中，將來式用現在式代替。

> We'll come to see you <u>if we have time</u>.
> 我們有時間會來看你。

> You'll catch the train <u>if you take a taxi</u>.
> 要是你搭計程車，還會趕得到火車。

> He will not leave <u>unless it is fine tomorrow</u>.
> 除非明天天晴，否則他不走。

Learn More

時間狀語從句也照這樣處理，例如：

> Tell him to wait <u>when he comes</u>.
> 他來了就讓他等着。

> Don't open the door <u>till the train stops</u>.
> 等火車停穩再開門。

5.16 表示 "現在之前"，ago 可用於現在完成式嗎？

✗ The artist **has died** fifty years **ago**, but he is still remembered by all.

✓ The artist **died** fifty years **ago**, but he is still remembered by all.

畫家五十年前死去，但大家仍記得他。

What's wrong?

錯誤有二：第一，"五十年前死去"發生在過去，指一個時間點，不能用現在完成式；第二，副詞 ago 不能與完成式連用。

> The story **took place** three years **ago**, but it remains fresh in my mind.
> 故事在三年前發生，但我依然記憶猶新。

Comparison

ago 指 "現在之前"，與過去式連用；before 指 "那時之前"，可與過去式或過去完成式連用。例如：

> They were divorced two years **ago**.
> 他們兩年前離了婚。

> It was fine yesterday, but it rained two days **before**.
> 昨天天晴，但兩天前下過雨。

> He told me that he had met Simon three weeks **before**.
> 他對我說，他三個星期前遇上西門。

5.17 表示 "非真實"，if-從句的動詞有何變化？

✗ If I <u>was</u> you, I would accept the job.

✓ If I <u>were</u> you, I would accept the job.

如果我是你，我會接受這份工作。

What's wrong?

從句是非真實條件句，第一人稱 I 的 be 動詞要用 were。又如：

If I <u>were</u> ten years younger, I would play football with you.

如果我年輕十歲，我會跟你們一起踢足球。

If I <u>were</u> in his place, I would think differently.

如果我處於他的位置，我考慮的就不同。

Comparison

事實上，不論甚麼人稱，be 動詞在非真實條件句中都用 were。例如：

If she <u>were</u> here, she would lend me a helping hand.

如果她在這裏，她會幫我。

If it <u>weren't</u> raining, we would dine out.

如果天不是正在下雨，我們會外出吃飯。

5.18 表示 "過去非真實"，主句的 can 和 will 有何變化？

✗ Without his help, I <u>cannot</u> succeed.

✓ Without his help, I <u>could not</u> have succeeded.

如果沒他幫忙，我本來不會成功。

What's wrong?

without his help 在本句相當於 if he had not helped me，是表示過去的非真實條件句，主句要用虛擬語氣。又如：

<u>Without</u> air and water, we <u>could</u> not exist.
要是沒有空氣和水，我們就無法生存。

He <u>would</u> not have become so rich <u>without</u> what his uncle had left to him.
要是沒有他叔叔留給他的那筆遺產，他不會變得那麼富有。

Grammar Rules

介詞短語常用作從句表達假設條件。例如：

<u>But for the floods</u>, the farmers <u>would</u> have yielded a better harvest.
要是沒有那場洪水，農民們的收成會好一些。

They could have won the game <u>under more favourable conditions</u>.
要是條件好一些，他們本來可以贏得比賽。

5.19 表示過去假設，用 if-從句要注意甚麼？

✗ My father <u>would not</u> die <u>if he listened to</u> the doctor's advice.

✓ My father would not <u>have died if he had listened to</u> the doctor's advice.

要是聽醫生勸告，我爸爸本來不會死。

What's wrong?

這句顯然是對過去的假設，因此要表示過去的虛擬形式，即從句是 "had + 過去分詞"，主句是 "would + have + 過去分詞"。又如：

The old man <u>would have been</u> 100 years old if he <u>had lived</u> ten more days.
要是能多活十天，那老人就到了 100 歲。

If I <u>had started</u> earlier, I <u>might not have missed</u> the train.
要是我早些出發，我也許不會錯過那班火車。

The cup <u>would have broken</u> if you <u>had not caught</u> it.
要是你沒有接住，這杯就會打破。

She <u>wouldn't have written</u> unless she <u>had heard</u> some news.
要是她沒聽到甚麼消息，她不會寫信來。

5.20 表示現在假設，用 if-從句要注意甚麼？

✗ Many dead <u>would</u> now <u>have been alive</u> if they had followed Dr Johnson's advice.

✓ Many dead <u>would</u> now <u>be alive</u> if they had followed Dr Johnson's advice.

許多去世的人，如能聽從約翰遜醫生的話去做，現在可能還活着。

What's wrong?

在這句中，主句含 now，表示現在假設，因此用 would (注意這與 5.19 主句表示過去假設不同)；if- 從句表示過去假設，因此用 if + 過去完成式。又如：

If I <u>had not been working</u> so hard in the past few months, things <u>would be</u> entirely <u>different</u> today.

要不是我過去幾個月努力工作，今天情況會完全不同。

If you <u>were</u> in good health, we <u>would have invited</u> you to the singing competition.

要是你健康還好，我們本來會邀請你參加歌唱比賽。

The rice <u>would be growing</u> better if there <u>had been</u> more rain.

要是雨下得多一點，水稻現在會長得更好。

5.21 表示要求，用 demand 可後跟 to-不定式嗎？

✗ The boss <u>demanded</u> Sam <u>to</u> send him the document by email.

✓ The boss <u>demanded</u> <u>that</u> Sam (should) send him the document by email.

老闆要求山姆電郵文件給他。

What's wrong?

動詞 demand 使用 "動詞 + 賓語從句" 句型，而賓語從句要用 "should + 動詞原形" 的形式，表示某事必須做或很重要，注意 should 可以省略。又如：

We <u>demanded</u> that another experiment (should) be made.
我們要求再做實驗一次。

Learn More

表示建議、命令、要求等的動詞，如 command、order、request、suggest 等，用法與 demand 相同。例如：

The major <u>ordered</u> Jack that his shoelaces (should) be done up.
少校命令傑克繫上鞋帶。

We <u>suggest</u> that the meeting (should) be postponed.
我們建議會議延期。

The landlady <u>requested</u> that he (should) pay the rent at once.
房東太太要求他馬上付房租。

Practice 練習 5

5.1 改正錯誤。

A

1. How dare you to talk to me like that?

   _____

2. Please pass the salt for me.

   _____

3. Wrote in 1939, the song is still very popular today.

   _____

4. To make greater progress, my father asked me to study harder.

   _____

5. On my way to work, I stopped mailing a letter.

   _____

6. Tom has gone to the library twice today.

   _____

7. Walking down the street, a bookstore was seen.

   _____

8. At the age of 6, his family left for Hong Kong.

   _____

B

1. He has come back just now.

   _____

2. We'll stay at home if it will rain tomorrow.

    _____

3. Our teacher told us that a good way to improve listening ability is to watch television.

    _____

4. When Columbus discovered America, he thought he arrived in India.

    _____

5. After discussed it with others, the boss accepted my proposal.

    _____

6. If the roads will not be improved soon, driving in this area becomes impossible.

    _____

7. If Susan would finish her thesis a little sooner, she would have gained her MA degree this summer.

    _____

8. He suggested me to apply to Oxford University.

    _____

5.2 選出正確答案。

1. The traffic accident <u>was happened / happened</u> just as I crossed the street.

2. There <u>has / have</u> to be at least six numbers or letters in the password.

3. We have no choice. We <u>must / may</u> go with mother.

4. Wait until the water <u>boils / boiling</u> before pouring it into the thermos.

5. We <u>stopped to talk / stopping to talk</u> to each other at the corner.

6. This note from the school needs <u>signing / to be signed</u> by your parents and then <u>returning / returned</u> to your teacher.

7. My baby sister <u>born / was born</u> in June last year.

8. John and Andy, but not Paul, <u>play / plays</u> basketball each day after school

9. I <u>didn't / don't</u> believe the time could go so fast.

10. We would have been there by now if you <u>had not lost / not lost</u> the map.

11. We urged the boy <u>should not touch / not to touch</u> the dead bird.

6. Adjectives
形容詞

6.1 形容詞最高級可用於兩者比較嗎?

✗ William is <u>the tallest</u> of the two boys.

✓ William is <u>the taller</u> of the two boys.

這兩個男孩之中,威廉個子高一些。

What's wrong?

這類句子,雖然不是 "A 比 B" 的形式,但仍是比較兩者,形容詞不能用最高級,而用比較級,並加定冠詞 the。

> Hers is <u>the poorer</u> of the two families.
> 她家是兩家人之中較窮的。

> This is <u>the less expensive</u> of the two bikes.
> 這是兩輛自行車中較便宜的一輛。

Grammar Rules

形容詞最高級用於比較三個或以上的人或物。

> Mary is <u>the eldest</u> of the three sisters.
> 瑪麗是三姐妹中最年長的一個。

> That is <u>the most reasonable</u> of all suggestions.
> 那是所有建議中最合理的一個。

6.2 表示"引人發笑"，用 amusing 還是 amused？

✗ The story was so <u>amused</u> that the children laughed a lot.

✓ The story was so <u>amusing</u> that the children laughed a lot.

這故事真有趣，孩子們開懷大笑。

What's wrong?

amused 和 amusing 是 amuse 的過去分詞和現在分詞。前者解作"覺得有趣"，一般修飾人；後者解作"有趣"、"令人發笑"，通常修飾事物。

> We are <u>amused</u> at the joke.
> 我們聽了這笑話覺得很有趣。

> It is an <u>amusing</u> joke.
> 這是個引人發笑的笑話。

Learn More

過去分詞和現在分詞的含義有以上差異的動詞很多，包括 amaze、annoy、astonish、disappoint、encourage、excite、exhaust、exhilarate、frighten、satisfy、shock。例如下列兩組例句：

> She feels greatly <u>encouraged</u> by her achievements.
> 她為自己的成就感到鼓舞。

> The early results are <u>encouraging</u>.
> 初步結果令人鼓舞。

> We are <u>shocked</u> at the news.
> 我們聽到這消息感到震驚。

> His behaviour at the party was <u>shocking</u>.
> 他在派對上的行為令人吃驚。

6.3 表示兩者對比，被比較之人或物該如何對應？

✗ <u>Bob's</u> house is much larger than <u>Tony</u>.

✓ <u>Bob's</u> house is much larger than <u>Tony's</u>.

鮑布的房子比東尼的大得多。

What's wrong?

兩者相比，要注意被比較之人或物彼此對應，house 不能與 Tony 相比。又如：

> <u>The new car</u> moves much faster than <u>the old one</u>.
> 新車比舊車跑得快多了。

> <u>He</u> received better language training than <u>I</u>.
> 他受過比我更好的語言訓練。

> It's warmer <u>today</u> than <u>yesterday</u>.
> 今天比昨天暖和。

> I like <u>him</u> more than <u>her</u>.
> 他和她相比，我更喜歡他。

6.4 形容詞用了比較級後還可加 less 或 more 嗎？

✗ This room is <u>less brighter</u> than that one.

✓ This room is <u>less bright</u> than that one.

這個房間不如那個明亮。

What's wrong?

"less + 形容詞原級" 已構成 "從低到高" 的比較級，形容詞本身無需再用比較級形式，否則就發生重複性錯誤。

> Susan is <u>less intelligent</u> than Mary.
> 蘇珊不如瑪麗聰明。

> The old car moves <u>less fast</u> than the new one.
> 那輛舊車不如這輛新車跑得快。

> This mobile phone is <u>less expensive</u> than that one.
> 這部手機比那部便宜。

Grammar Rules

同樣，在 "從高到低" 的比較級中，用了 more 之後，形容詞本身不能再用比較級形式，反之亦然，形容詞用了比較級形式之後不能再用 more。例如：

> Susan is <u>younger</u> than Mary.
> 蘇珊比瑪麗年紀小。

> This question is <u>more difficult</u> than that one.
> 這個問題比那個困難。

6.5 表示 "比某人優越"，用 superior 還要加 more 嗎？

✗ Some whites think that they are more <u>superior than</u> the blacks.

✓ Some whites think that they are <u>superior to</u> the blacks.

有些白人認為自己比黑人優越。

What's wrong?

superior 是個特殊的形容詞，它本身就是比較級形式，前面不加 more，後面不跟 than，但需要介詞 to。

He is clearly superior to all the other players.
他顯然比所有其他球員優秀。

She is superior to him in the company.
她在公司裏職位比他高。

Learn More

inferior、junior、senior、prior 與 superior 的性質相同。例如：

Women are not <u>inferior to</u> men.
女人不比男人低等。

This civilization is by far <u>junior to</u> that of the Yellow River Valley.
這種文明遠遠晚於黃河流域文明。

Practice is <u>prior to</u> theory.
實踐先於理論。

6.6 含複合形容詞的 well，最高級要加 most 嗎？

✗ The woman is the most <u>well-known</u> figure in the village.

✓ The woman is the <u>best-known</u> figure in the village.

那個女人是村裏最有名的人物。

What's wrong?

由 "well + 分詞" 構成的複合形容詞，它的比較級及最高級形式按副詞 well 的變化規則變化。

> This country has a <u>better-disciplined</u> army than that one.
> 這國比那國擁有一支更精銳的軍隊。
>
> She is looking for a <u>better-paid</u> job.
> 她正在找一份更高薪的工作。
>
> He is the <u>best-informed</u> person in this group.
> 他是這群人中消息最靈通的人。

Grammar Rules

英語中複合形容詞甚多，有由 "副詞 + 分詞" 構成、也有由 "形容詞 + 分詞" 構成，大多沒有比較級或最高級，若有比較級或最高級，會按副詞或形容詞的規則而變化。例如：

> She is <u>better-looking</u> than her sister.
> 她長得比她妹妹漂亮。

6.7 三者比較時,形容詞可用比較級嗎?

✗ Who is <u>taller</u>, John, William or Tom?

✓ Who is <u>the tallest</u>, John, William or Tom?

誰個子高一些,約翰、威廉還是湯姆?

What's wrong?

這是個有三個對象的選擇疑問句,實際上是比較三者。比較和選擇三個或以上對象時,形容詞要用最高級。又如:

Which novel by Dickens is <u>the most interesting</u>, *Oliver Twist*, *David Copperfield* or *A Tale of Two Cities*?

狄更斯寫的哪本小說更有意思,《苦海孤雛》、《塊肉餘生記》或《雙城記》?

如果只有兩個選擇對象,就應用形容詞比較級:

Who is <u>taller</u>, John or William?

誰個子高一些,約翰或威廉?

Which novel by Dickens is <u>more interesting</u>, *Oliver Twist* or *A Tale of Two Cities*?

狄更斯寫的哪本小說更有意思,《苦海孤雛》或《雙城記》?

6.8 表示"長期健康",用 healthy 還是 well?

✗ I hope you feel <u>more healthy</u> today.

✓ I hope you feel <u>better</u> today.

希望你今天感覺好一點。

What's wrong?

healthy 和 well 都表示"身體好"、"健康",但 healthy 是指長期的健康,well 是指某個特定時刻的健康。"今天"是個特定時刻,因此這句只能用 well 的比較級。比較:

Mary looks very <u>healthy</u>.
瑪麗看上去很健康。

His father was not so <u>well</u> yesterday.
他父親昨天不大舒服。

My mother is <u>healthier</u> than ever before.
我母親比過去任何時候都健康。

He is getting <u>better</u> now.
他正在康復。

Grammar Tips

一般情況下 **well** 只用作表語,**healthy** 還可用作定語:
Mary is a <u>healthy</u> girl.
瑪麗是個健康女孩。

6.9 表示 "害怕"，在名詞前可用 afraid 嗎？

✗ The <u>afraid</u> child ran into the house.

✓ The <u>frightened</u> child ran into the house.

那嚇着了的孩子跑進屋裏。

What's wrong?

afraid 只能用在名詞之後，不能在名詞之前用作定語，frightened 可以出現在兩種位置。比較：

The deer seems dreadfully <u>afraid</u> / <u>frightened</u>.
那鹿似乎怕得厲害。

The <u>frightened</u> deer was hiding in the bush.
那受驚的鹿躲在灌木叢裏。

Grammar Rules

有些形容詞像 afraid 一樣，不能在名詞之前用作定詞，如 alive、alone、asleep、ill，這時要用相應的其他形容詞 (如 living、lonely、sleeping、sick)。例如以下兩組句子：

Is the old man still <u>alive</u> / <u>living</u>?
那老人還活着嗎？

Does the old man have any <u>living</u> relatives?
那老人還有活着的親屬嗎？

My grandmother is <u>ill</u> / <u>sick</u>.
我祖母病了。

The <u>sick</u> baby died yesterday.
那個生病的嬰孩昨天死了。

6.10 用 man 或 woman 表示複數名詞的性別時，動詞會用複數嗎？

✗ Two <u>man doctors</u> and three <u>woman nurses</u> work in the clinic.

✓ Two <u>men doctors</u> and three <u>women nurses</u> work in the clinic.

兩名男醫生和三名女護士在這診所工作。

What's wrong?

用 man 或 woman 修飾可數名詞以顯示性別，要隨名詞數的變化而變化。

Susan has many <u>men</u> friends.
蘇珊有許多男性朋友。

This restaurant is in need of some <u>women</u> cooks.
這間餐廳需要一些女廚師。

She became the first <u>woman</u> writer in the town.
她成為該市第一個女作家。

Our school has two <u>men</u> teachers.
我們學校有兩名男教師。

Grammar Tips

已形成複合詞的詞語就無需作這種變化，例如：

a girlfriend ⟶ two girlfriends
一個女朋友　　兩個女朋友

a she-goat ⟶ three she-goats
一隻母山羊　　三隻母山羊

Practice 練習 6

6.1 改正錯誤。

1. The river is nearly 100 metre wide.

    _____

2. My sister's new bike costs more than Mary.

    _____

3. She is the tallest of the twin sisters.

    _____

4. Tom seems to be a more ill-informed person than
    Jane.

    _____

5. My sister is three years elder than I.

    _____

6. My computer is much more inferior than yours.

    _____

7. The speech was so bored that we didn't want to
    listen any more.

    _____

8. The more they talked, the more encouraging they
    felt.

    _____

6.2 在正確句子前面加 ✓ 。

___ There are the toilets. On the right is the woman.
     On the left is the man.

___ There are the toilets. On the right is the women's.

On the left is the men's.

___ My very tall cousin is actually younger than me.

___ My very tall cousin is actually young than me.

___ My dog is better trained than your dog.

___ My dog is more trained than your dog.

___ Ask the librarian. She is the well-informed person in the whole school.

___ Ask the librarian. She is the best-informed person in the whole school.

___ We have tickets for front row seats. I'm so exciting!

___ We have tickets for front row seats. I'm so excited!

___ Comparing Hong Kong, Guangzhou and Shanghai, Guangzhou has the smaller population.

___ Comparing Hong Kong, Guangzhou and Shanghai, Guangzhou has the smallest population.

___ That computer is the most least expensive.

___ That computer is the least expensive.

___ Hey! Why does Jack have a more bigger piece of cake than I have?

___ Hey! Why does Jack have a bigger piece of cake than I have?

___ Let sleeping dogs lie.

___ Let asleep dogs lie.

___ You would do well to get more exercise and fresh air.

___ You would do good to get more exercise and fresh air.

7. Adverbs
副詞

7.1 表示程度時，very 可直接修飾動詞嗎？

✗ I <u>very</u> <u>love</u> my parents.

✓ I <u>love</u> my parents <u>very</u> much.

我很愛我父母。

What's wrong?

副詞 very 不能直接修飾動詞，必須跟其他副詞構成副詞詞組以表示程度，而且常置於動詞之後。

> We like the movie <u>very</u> much.
> 我們很喜歡這部電影。

> He has been working <u>very</u> hard these days.
> 他近來工作一直很努力。

> She always listens <u>very</u> carefully in class.
> 她上課總是很仔細聽講。

> **Grammar Tips**
> **very** 可直接修飾形容詞或副詞以表示程度。例如：
> Time passes <u>very</u> quickly.
> 時間過得很快。
> It is a <u>very</u> exciting event.
> 這是一個非常令人興奮的活動。

7.2 hardly 能與 not 連用嗎？

✗ She did <u>not</u> <u>hardly</u> wait to hear the news.

✓ She could <u>hardly</u> wait to hear the news.

她等不及要聽那消息。

What's wrong?

副詞 hardly 本身含否定意思，不能和 not 連用。它常置於 can 或 could 與主動詞之間以強調難度。

Speak louder — I can <u>hardly</u> hear you.
講大聲些 —— 我幾乎聽不到你在說甚麼。
<u>Hardly</u> a question could she answer.
她幾乎連一個問題也答不到。

Learn More

與 hardly 同類的還有 barely、scarcely、rarely，用法與 hardly 相似。例如：

He was so tired that he could <u>barely</u> stand up.
他累得幾乎站不起來。

You can <u>scarcely</u> expect me to believe you.
你休想我相信你的話。

People can <u>rarely</u> live to 100.
人很難活到 100 歲。

7.3 表示"花了一些時間"，用 sometime 還是 some time？

✗ I've spent <u>sometime</u> on this book.

✓ I've spent <u>some time</u> on this book.
我在這本書上已花了一些時間。

What's wrong?

sometime 不是代詞，而是副詞，意思是"將來某個時候"，如 I'll speak to him about it sometime.（我以後會找他談談這件事。）。表示"一些時間"用 some time，如：

That year, I stayed with my aunt for <u>some time</u>.
那年我在姨媽家裏住了一段時間。

Grammar Rules

要提防使用類似結構時出錯。看下列兩組例句：

I must have <u>some place</u> to put my books.
我必須有個放書的地方。

My uncle lives <u>someplace</u> else.
我叔叔住在別處。

We have to find <u>some way</u> to solve the problem.
我們要找些方法解決問題。

She solved the problem <u>someway</u>.
她以某種辦法解決了問題。

7.4 表示 "不喜歡…也不喜歡"，可用 too 嗎？

✗ He doesn't know the answer, but I don't, <u>too</u>.

✓ He doesn't know the answer, but I don't, <u>either</u>.

他不知道答案，我也不知道。

What's wrong?

副詞 too 用於肯定句，否定句要用 either，通常置於句尾。比較下列兩組例子：

I like gardening and she does <u>too</u>.
我喜歡園藝，她也喜歡。
I don't like gardening and she doesn't <u>either</u>.
我不喜歡園藝，她也不喜歡。

She is very wise and he is <u>too</u>.
她很明智，他也是。
She is not very wise and he is not <u>either</u>.
她不很明智，他也是。

Learn More

also 是 too 的同義詞，也不用於否定句，但在句中的位置不同，通常在實義動詞之前或 be 動詞之後。also 主要用於正式場合及書面語。例如：

Mary <u>also</u> likes cooking. 瑪麗也喜歡做飯。
She is <u>also</u> very wise. 她也很明智。

7.5 表示"剛才"，just 可用於過去式嗎？

✗ I <u>have seen</u> her <u>just now</u>.

✓ I <u>have just seen</u> her.

✓ I <u>saw</u> her <u>just now</u>.

我剛看到她。

What's wrong?

副詞 just 和 just now 都有"剛才"、"方才"、"剛剛"的意思，即 only a short time ago。但 just now 解作"剛才"時，只能用於過去式，just 用作"剛才"時，必須和現在完成式連用。比較下列幾組句子：

He has <u>just</u> left for Hangzhou.
He left for Hangzhou <u>just now</u>.
他剛去了杭州。

I have <u>just</u> heard the news.
I heard the news <u>just now</u>.
我剛聽到這個消息。

另外，兩者在詞序上略有差別，just now 一般置於句尾，而 just 置於助動詞 have / had 與主動詞之間。

7.6 表示 "尤其是"，用 specially 還是 especially？

✗ She is <u>specially</u> interested in music.

✓ She is <u>especially</u> interested in music.

她尤其對音樂感興趣。

What's wrong?

especially 和 specially 都是形容詞 special 的副詞，但意義不同。前者意思是 in particular / particularly（尤其，特別），後者意思是 for a particular purpose（專門）。比較：

Tom likes fruit, <u>especially</u> apples and peaches.
湯姆愛吃水果，尤其是蘋果和桃。

Tom is eating a big apple <u>specially</u> bought for him.
湯姆吃着專為他買的一個大蘋果。

She loves to wear a skirt, <u>especially</u> a red one.
她愛穿裙子，尤其是紅色的裙。

She wears a skirt <u>specially</u> made in town.
她穿着一條專門在城裏做的裙子。

> **Grammar Tips**
> 英式英語中，**especially** 和 **specially** 可替換使用。

7.7 表示 "回家"，用 go home 還是 go to home?

✗ It's getting late. I'd better <u>go to home</u>.

✓ It's getting late. I'd better <u>go home</u>.

天晚了。我該回家。

What's wrong?

home 指自己的家，總是不帶 to。

It's time to go <u>home</u>. 該回家了。

When did you get <u>home</u> yesterday?
你昨天甚麼時候回家?

home 還用作副詞，直接跟在動詞之後。

He arrived <u>home</u> at 3 this afternoon.
他今午 3 點鐘回家。

I'd rather stay <u>home</u> on Sundays.

我星期天寧可留在家裏。

Learn More

home 可與物主代詞連用，也可有修飾成分，這時的
用法與普通名詞相同。例如：

My <u>home</u> is in Madrid.
我家在馬德里。

This old house would make an ideal <u>home</u>.
這老房子可以成為一個理想的家。

7.8 表示強調，用 such 與 many 一起修飾名詞嗎？

✗ I had <u>such many</u> clothes to wash last Sunday.

✓ I had <u>so many</u> clothes to wash last Sunday.

上星期天我有那麼多衣服要洗。

What's wrong?

such 修飾名詞，so 修飾形容詞或副詞。此句強調具有形容詞性質的 many，不是強調名詞 clothes，因此用 so。比較：

The eagle flies at <u>such</u> a speed. 鷹飛得真快。
The eagle flies <u>so</u> fast. 鷹飛得真快。

Tom is <u>such</u> a bore. 湯姆這人真悶。
The book is <u>so</u> boring. 這本書真沒意思。

Grammar Rules

如果名詞之前帶有冠詞及形容詞，要根據強調對象決定用 such 或 so，有時還要調整詞序。例如：

It is <u>such</u> a boring movie. (強調名詞)
這真是一部無聊的電影。

It is <u>so</u> boring a movie (= The movie is so boring). (強調形容詞)
這部電影真無聊。

7.9 表示 "後者",用 latter 還是 later?

✗ She was a doctor but <u>latter</u> turned to literature.

✓ She was a doctor but <u>later</u> turned to literature.

她是一名醫生,但後來改為從事文學。

What's wrong?

latter 和 later 只有一個字母之差,樣子相似,但意思完全不同,詞性也不同。latter 是形容詞,the latter 指兩者之 "後者",在句中起名詞作用,例如:

Will and Bill are brothers, but the former is much more intelligent than <u>the latter</u>.
威爾和比爾是兄弟,但前者比後者聰明得多。

later 是副詞,意思是 "後來"、"以後",用作狀語,例如:

Bill graduated from London University in 1999. <u>Later</u>, he joined the army.
比爾 1999 年畢業於倫敦大學。後來他參了軍。

They fell in love at first sight. <u>Later</u>, they got married.
他們一見鍾情。後來,他們結了婚。

> **Grammar Tips**
> later 是 late 的比較級形式,latter 不是。

7.10 表示 "到底" ，用 wherever 或 where ever ？

✗ **Wherever** could I have lost the key?

✓ **Where ever** could I have lost the key?

我到底會把鑰匙丟在哪裏？

What's wrong?

wherever 和 where ever 樣子相似，只是後者沒有連寫。但 wherever 是連接詞，意思是 "無論在哪裏" ，用以引出一個從句。例如：

Wherever you go, I will go. 你去哪裏，我也去哪裏。

where 是副詞，ever 表示強調，意思是 "到底" 、 "究竟" ，跟 wherever 意思不同。例如：

Where ever could the dog have gone?
這狗到底跑到哪裏去呢？

Comparison

ever 可與強調疑問代詞及疑問副詞連用，如 who ever 、 what ever 、 why ever 、 how ever 等形似連接詞 whoever 、 whatever 、 whyever 、 however ，必須要注意上述不同之處。

Whenever he coughs, he feels a good deal of pain.
每次咳嗽時，他都痛得厲害。

When ever did he leave home?
他到底是甚麼時候離家的？

However bad the weather may be, we must start off tomorrow. 無論天氣多壞，我們明天必須出發。

How ever did they accomplish the task ahead of time? 他們到底用了甚麼方法提前完成任務？

Practice 練習 7

7.1 改正錯誤。

1. John very love Mary.

   _____

2. They can't hardly speak English.

   _____

3. This skirt is especially designed for you.

   _____

4. The flowers in the garden are such beautiful.

   _____

5. However did he manage to find the lost wallet?

   _____

6. Three hours latter, they returned safe and sound.

   _____

7. The cave is almost 100 metres deep.

   _____

8. He loves music and she does either.

   _____

7.2 改正錯誤。

1. I didn't barely recognize him.

2. If you're not going, then I am not going too.

3. Do I have to? This practice is just such boring.

4. Are you boring? Playing a video game would be such more interesting, right?

5. Wash your hands before you do anything, specially if

you've been outside playing.

6. Put the ladder against the wall and latter we can climb up and clean the windows.

7. I haven't seen my grandmother for sometime.

8. Here is a menu. You can order what ever you want.

9. Listen! I heard just now a bird singing.

10. He very speaks English well and works as a translator.

8. Prepositions
介詞

8.1 表示 "被動語態"，還保留短語動詞的介詞嗎？

✗ Old people in China <u>are taken good care</u>.

✓ Old people in China <u>are taken good care of</u>.

中國的老年人受到很好的照顧。

What's wrong?

這句的主動語態是：(The government) takes good care of old people in China. 原句有 of，在被動語態中不能省略 of。

Learn More

在被動語態中，要提防忘掉原有短語動詞內的介詞。例如：

> What is the table made <u>of</u>?
> 這桌子用甚麼材料製造？
>
> The children are well looked <u>after</u>.
> 孩子們受到很好的照顧。
>
> The lost time must be made up <u>for</u>.
> 失去的時間一定要追回來。
>
> The foolish girl is looked down <u>upon</u>.
> 這傻女孩給人看不起。
>
> This noise cannot be put up <u>with</u>.
> 這噪音令人無法忍受。

8.2 在定語從句中，不及物動詞後接 which 嗎？

✗ This is the house <u>which I once lived</u>.

✓ This is the house <u>which I once lived in</u>.

這是我以前住過的房子。

What's wrong?

live 是不及物動詞，無法跟代詞 which 發生關係，必須保留原有的介詞 in。

Learn More

這種情況常發生在定語從句中。例如：

The day <u>on which</u> I met my future wife was the greatest in my life.
我遇見我未來妻子的那天，是我一生中最美好的一天。

His father is a man <u>on whom</u> you can safely depend.
他父親是你完全可以信賴的人。

Is this the key you have been looking <u>for</u>?
這就是你一直在找的鑰匙嗎？

Do you know the girl (whom) Jack is talking <u>to</u>?
你認不認識正在和傑克講話的那個女孩？

8.3 and 共有的賓語有不同介詞時，可省略介詞嗎？

✗ She has <u>a need and an interest in</u> music.

✓ She has <u>a need for and an interest in</u> music.

她對音樂有需要，也有興趣。

What's wrong?

一個句子有兩個或以上部分 (如上句中的 have a need 及 have an interest) 共享一個賓語 (如上句中的 music)，而所需的介詞各不相同 (如上句中的 for 及 in)，或者後面部分是及物動詞，那前面部分的介詞 (如上句中的 for) 就不可以省去。

Learn More

這種情況主要發生於含並列謂語的句子中。例如：

He <u>takes an active part in</u> and enjoys these recreational activities.
他不但積極參予，也很喜歡這些文娛活動。

Mary <u>has great respect for</u> and often pays a visit to that old writer.
瑪麗對那個老作家懷有深切敬意，並經常拜訪他。

She <u>is very patient with</u> and never lays a finger on the children.
她對孩子們很有耐性，從不傷害他們。

8.4 表示 "下午" ，afternoon 何時用 in，何時用 on？

✗ The meeting was held <u>in the afternoon</u> of May 20.

✓ The meeting was held <u>on the afternoon</u> of May 20.

會議在 5 月 20 日下午舉行。

What's wrong?

afternoon 一般與 in 連用，如 I usually take a walk in the afternoon.（我通常在下午散步一會。），又如 She died at 3 in the afternoon.（她下午三點去世。）但如果指某個特定的下午，介詞就必須用 on。

> Professor Harold is to give us a talk <u>on Monday afternoon</u>.
> 哈羅德教授定於星期一下午為我們演講。
> I arrived <u>on a hot June afternoon</u>.
> 我在六月一個炎熱的下午到達。

Learn More

morning、evening 用法相同。例如：

> <u>On a chilly winter morning</u>, I said goodbye to my beloved hometown.
> 在一個寒冷的冬日上午，我告別了我熱愛的故鄉。

Grammar Tips
this morning、**tomorrow afternoon**、**yesterday evening** 不用介詞。

8.5 表示 "長在樹上" 用 in 嗎?

✗ Listen! A bird is singing <u>on the tree</u>.

✓ Listen! A bird is singing <u>in the tree</u>.

聽! 有一隻鳥在樹上歌唱。

What's wrong?

on the tree 的意思是長在樹上,in the tree 的意思是停在樹上,四周有樹葉遮擋,似在裏面,所在這句應用 in。比較:

Our cat is playing <u>in the tree</u>.
我家的貓在樹上玩。

Money does not grow <u>on trees</u>.
諺語:錢不是樹上長出來的 / 錢來之不易。

Learn More

street、mountain 用法相似。例如:

She came across an old classmate of hers <u>in the street</u>.
她在街上遇到她一個老同學。

I dare not walk alone <u>in the mountains</u>.
我不敢一個人在山上走。

8.6 表示 "超過某數量" 用 above 嗎？

✗ In the United States, people of 65 and <u>above</u> are called senior citizens.

✓ In the United States, people of 65 and <u>over</u> are called senior citizens.

在美國，65 歲及以上的人被稱為長者。

What's wrong?

表示數量時，above 側重方向，over 側重 "多於"、"超過"。比較：

The mountain is 3,000 metres <u>above</u> sea level.
這山海拔 3,000 米。

<u>Over</u> 20 heads of state attended the conference.
二十多個國家元首出席了大會。

The temperature suddenly dropped to 5 degrees <u>above</u> zero.
氣溫突然降到五度。

The President talked <u>over</u> 2 hours.
總統講了兩個多小時。

海拔和氣溫有縱向之感，故用 above.

> **Grammar Tips**
> 表示年齡時，有人不太嚴格，常見到 **above** 和 **over** 混用，如：**people aged 50 and above / over**（50 歲及以上的人）。

8.7 如何用 such 表示程度？

✗ My friend treated me <u>such to</u> a rich dinner.

✓ My friend treated me to <u>such</u> a rich dinner.

我朋友招待我吃了一頓很豐富的晚餐。

What's wrong?

such 不可置於介詞之前，必須緊跟 a/an，形成 "such + a/an + 形容詞 + 名詞" 的結構。又如：

He is assigned to <u>such an</u> interesting job.
他獲分配做一項很有意思的工作。

John came out with <u>such a</u> strange plan.
約翰提出了一項很奇特的計劃。

> **Grammar Tips**
>
> 這個結構表示程度，常與 **that** 連用以表示結果：
>
> It was <u>such</u> a beautiful night <u>that</u> she wanted to take a walk.
> 晚上景色很美，她想出去散散步。
>
> Grandma told us <u>such an</u> interesting story <u>that</u> we all laughed.
> 祖母給我們講了一個十分有趣的故事，逗得我們全都大笑起來。

8.8 表示 "三個或以上的人或物" 用 between 嗎？

✗ It's a secret <u>among</u> us two.

✓ It's a secret <u>between</u> us two.

這是我們兩人之間的秘密。

What's wrong?

between 常用於兩個人或物之間，among 總是用於三個或以上的人或物之間。比較：

Jack and Mary had no ill feeling <u>between</u> them.
傑克和瑪麗之間沒有猜忌。

We divided up the chocolates <u>among</u> three of us.
我們三個人分了朱古力。

Aunt Polly sat <u>between</u> the bed and the door.
波莉姨姨坐在牀和門之間。

I found the missing photo <u>among</u> a heap of old greeting cards.
我在一大堆舊賀卡裏找到那張丟失的照片。

> **Grammar Tips**
> 三者或以上若被當作是一組，講的是兩組之間的關係，也可用 **between**。例如：
> Do you know the difference <u>between</u> wheat, leek and green onion?
> 你分得清小麥、韭菜和嫩洋葱嗎？

8.9 表示 "圍着桌子坐" 用 sit on 嗎?

✗ Eight people <u>sat on</u> the table.

✓ Eight people <u>sat at</u> the table.

那張餐桌上坐着八個人。

What's wrong?

"上" 是中文的概念。八個人圍着一張餐桌吃飯,不可能真的坐在桌子上面,因此不可用 on,而要用 at。

Grammar Rules

許多 "上" 的概念不能用 on,而要根據習慣使用其他介詞。例如:

The old temple is situated <u>at</u> the top of the hill.
古廟位於山頂上。

There is an eagle's nest <u>in</u> the oak tree.
橡樹上有個老鷹窩。

She was ill and lay <u>in</u> bed.
她病了,躺在牀上。

They accepted the agreement <u>in</u> principle.
他們原則上接受這個協議。

8.10 表示 "水平線上的一點" 用 in 嗎？

✗ A big dam will be built <u>in the river</u>.

✓ A big dam will be built <u>on the river</u>.

那條河上將建一座大壩。

What's wrong?

雖然大壩建在水裏，但不可用 in。凡表示平面或線上的一點，介詞都要用 on。河被視為一條線，壩是線上的一點，因此是 on the river。又如：

Wuhan is a city <u>on</u> the Yangtze River.
武漢位於長江上。

Several small islands are visible <u>on</u> the sea.
海面上可見幾個小島。

Many fishing boats are sailing <u>on</u> the lake.
許多漁船在湖面上揚帆航行。

A new petrol station was set up <u>on</u> the motorway.
高速公路上新建了一個加油站。

8.11 表示"遞某物給某人"用 for 嗎?

✗ After she run for 100 metres, she <u>passed the stick for</u> the next runner.

✓ After she ran for 100 metres, she <u>passed the stick to</u> the next runner.

她跑完 100 米後,便將接力棒交給下一名選手。

What's wrong?

及物動詞 pass 的間接賓語後置時,介詞用 to,不用 for。

Please pass the salt <u>to</u> me.
請遞鹽給我。

Learn More

間接賓語後置時,用 to 的動詞很多,包括 bring、hand、leave、lend、offer、owe、pay、read、return、send、sell、show、take、teach、tell、throw、write。

He <u>offered</u> a cigarette <u>to</u> her.
他敬她一支香煙。

She <u>has returned</u> the book <u>to</u> the library.
她已將書還給圖書館。

Please <u>read</u> the story <u>to</u> me.
請讀這故事給我聽。

8.12 表示 "為某人做事" 用 to 嗎？

✗ She <u>made an overcoat to</u> him.

✓ She <u>made an overcoat for</u> him.

她為他做了一件大衣。

What's wrong?

及物動詞 make 的間接賓語後置時，介詞用 for，不用 to。

The mother <u>made a toy for</u> her baby.
媽媽為嬰孩自製了一件玩具。

Learn More

間接賓語後置時，用 for 的動詞很多，包括 buy、do、fix、leave、order、save、spare。

John <u>fixed the bike for</u> Mary.
約翰為瑪麗修理好自行車。

He <u>ordered a beer for</u> himself.
他自己要了一杯啤酒。

Can you <u>spare a few minutes for</u> me?
你能為我抽出幾分鐘時間嗎？

Practice 練習 8

8.1 改正錯誤。

1. Look! There are two monkeys on the trees.

   _____

2. When you move to a new place, it takes a lot
   of getting used.

   _____

3. The new theatre was inaugurated in the afternoon
   of May 23, 2001.

   _____

4. She participated and learned much from
   the seminar.

   _____

5. I'll never forget the day which I joined the army.

   _____

6. It was liver cancer that his grandfather died.

   _____

7. It's easy to make friends with people as him.

   _____

8. Finally we saw a house between the trees.

   _____

8.2 用 **at**、**on**、**of**、**in** 填空。

I want you to meet me _____ noon, _____ the corner of
Nathan Road and Jordan Road. Get _____ bus number
2 _____ the Star Ferry Pier terminus and get off after

6 stops. I suggest first we go _____ the big department store _____ the corner and look _____ the display _____ Chinese arts and handicrafts _____ the 4th floor.

8.3 用 like、as 填空。

1. Our school has no sports ground _____ theirs.

2. My dog understands my moods _____ if he can read my mind.

3. This bed is so comfortable, it is _____ sleeping on a cloud.

4. Treat others _____ you would like them to treat you.

5. To get the job done we need to work together _____ a team.

8.4 用 between、among 填空。

1. I'm trying to find a small key _____ all the junk in my desk drawer.

2. The coin fell _____ the two cushions on the couch.

8.5 用 above、over 填空。

1. The atmosphere _____ the earth's surface is about 1,000 km thick.

2. If you keep eating like that you are going to weigh _____ 100 kg!

9. Linking Words
連詞

9.1 用 **and** 表示 "諸如此類"，是否後接 **so on**？

✗ There is a similar custom in many countries, for example in Britain and France, <u>etc.</u>

✓ There is a similar custom in many countries, <u>for example</u> in Britain and France.

許多國家有類似習俗，比如英國和法國。

What's wrong?

用於連接兩個或以上相同的句子成分，置於最後兩個成分之間，表示已完結，不可再後接 and so on、and so forth、etc. (= and so forth)，尤其在舉例時。比較：

The store sells pencils, paper and calculators.
這間商店出售鉛筆、紙張和計算機。

The store sells pencils, paper, calculators <u>and so on</u>.
這間商店出售鉛筆、紙張、計算機等。

She is interested in music <u>and</u> sports.
她對音樂和體育感興趣。

She is interested in music, sports, <u>etc.</u>
她對音樂、體育等感興趣。

There are many interesting places to visit around here—the zoo and the museum <u>for instance</u>.
這一帶有許多有意思的地方可去 —— 比如動物園和博物館。

There are many interesting places to visit around here—the zoo, the museum <u>and so forth</u>.
這一帶有許多有意思的地方可去 —— 比如動物園、博物館等。

9.2 表示 "因為…所以"，可同時用 because 和 so 嗎？

✗ <u>Because</u> it is raining, <u>so</u> the basketball match is cancelled.

✓ <u>Because</u> it is raining, the basketball match is cancelled.

因為天在下雨，所以籃球賽取消了。

What's wrong?

中文常說 "因為…所以…"，誤句是中英對號入座而引起錯誤。because 是從屬連詞，so 是並列連詞，兩者只可用其一，不可同時用。

英文中 "因為…所以…" 不可用兩個詞語表達，用其中之一即可。例如：

We couldn't drive fast <u>because</u> / <u>as</u> the road was slippery. (從屬連詞)
因為路很滑，所以我們車子開不快。

It was getting dark, so we decided to go home. (並列連詞)
因為天色漸暗，所以我們決定回家。

We didn't go for a walk, <u>for</u> it was raining. (並列連詞)
因為天在下雨，所以我們沒有去散步。

It is cold, <u>therefore</u> we should wear more. (並列連詞)
因為天氣冷，所以我們要多穿衣服。

9.3 表示 "雖然…但是", 可同時用 though 和 but 嗎?

✗ <u>Though</u> he is ill, <u>but</u> he has still gone to school.

✓ <u>Though</u> he is ill, he has still gone to school.
雖然他病了,但他還是去上學。

What's wrong?

中文常説 "雖然…但是…",誤句是中英對號入座而引起錯誤。Though / although 是從屬連詞,but 是並列連詞,兩者只能用其一,不可同時使用。在英文中,表達 "雖然…但是…" 不會用兩個詞語,只用其中之一就可以。例如:

> <u>Though</u> / <u>Although</u> the weather was bad, the satellite was successfully launched. (從屬連詞)
> 雖然天氣很差,但衛星仍成功發射。

> It was extremely windy, <u>but</u> the space shuttle landed safely.
> 雖然風很大,但航天飛機仍安全着陸。

> There was a virus infection, <u>yet</u> all the documents in the computer were restored.
> 雖然感染了病毒,但電腦裏所有文件都恢復了。

> **Grammar Tips**
> 有時 **though** 與 **yet** 連用,但這種情況下的 **yet** 是副詞。

9.4 表示 "直到…時候"，如何用 until？

✗ They arrived here <u>until</u> midnight.

✓ They did not arrive here <u>until</u> midnight.

他們半夜才到達這裏。

What's wrong?

誤句不能成立。從屬連詞 until 或 till 的意思是：直到…時候，主句的行為結束。"他們沒有到達這裏。"的行為到半夜結束，也就是說，"他們半夜才到達這裏"。又如：

The library is open <u>until</u> / <u>till</u> 6 p.m.
圖書館下午 6 點鐘關門。

She stood there <u>until</u> / <u>till</u> the train was out of sight.
直到火車消失她才離開那裏。

<u>Until</u> I told him, he knew nothing about the accident.
等我告訴了他，他才知道這宗事故。

They did not find the dog <u>until</u> the next day.
他們第二天才找到那隻狗。

9.5 表示 "連接三部分"，要用兩次 or 嗎？

✗ <u>Either</u> Jack or Susan <u>or</u> Mary will help you.

✓ <u>Either</u> Jack, Susan <u>or</u> Mary will help you.

✓ Jack, Susan <u>or</u> Mary will help you.

傑克、蘇珊或瑪麗會幫你。

What's wrong?

並列連詞常連接兩個等同部分，例如：

> You can come <u>either</u> tomorrow <u>or</u> the day after tomorrow.
> 你可以明天或後天來。

> <u>Either</u> my father <u>or</u> my mother will pick you up.
> 我爸或我媽會開車接你。

連接三部分或以上也是可以的，但不必每部分都用 or，只要最後兩部分用 or 連接即可。又如：

> You can go there either by bus, by underground <u>or</u> by taxi.
> 你可以搭巴士、地鐵或計程車到那裏。

這種情況下，最好刪去 either，變成：You can go there by bus, by underground <u>or</u> by taxi. 。

9.6 何時用 because，何時用 because of？

✗ <u>Because of</u> he worked very hard this term, he passed the exam easily.

✓ <u>Because</u> he worked very hard this term, he passed the exam easily.

由於他這學期很努力，他輕鬆通過了考試。

What's wrong?

because of 是介詞，不是連詞，因此不能引導從句，只能構成介詞短語，例如：

> The football match was cancelled <u>because of</u> rain.
> 球賽因下雨而取消了。

> The old lady is blind <u>because of</u> cataracts.
> 那老太太因患白內障而失明。

Learn More

常被誤用的另一個介詞是 despite。despite 和 in spite of 的意思是 "即使"，也只可構成介詞短語。例如：

> <u>In spite of</u> rain, the match was held as planned.
> 即使下雨，比賽仍按計劃進行。

有時 despite 後加 the fact that，可以引出從句，例如：

> <u>Despite the fact that</u> he was seriously ill, he persisted in writing his novel.
> 即使他病得很重，他仍堅持寫他的小說。

Practice 練習 9

9.1 改正錯誤。

1. While she was in college, she learned both English as well as French.

   _____

2. Because of he was ill, he did not go to school yesterday.

   _____

3. Though he worked hard, but the boss fired him.

   _____

4. Tom behaved so badly at the party as nobody liked him.

   _____

5. The rain stopped until noon.

   _____

6. You may come either by bike and on foot.

   _____

7. Because he studied well this term, so he passed the exam easily.

   _____

8. Despite it was raining, we worked three hours in the field.

   _____

9.2 改正錯誤。

1. I like all kinds of ball games, for example soccer, volleyball, etc.

2. Because my watch stopped so I was late.

3. You left your bag unattended yet it was stolen.

4. Pat did not study at all so she still scored well on the test.

5. Because of I watched a scary movie, I could not go to sleep.

6. We had to choose between either shopping or watching a movie or going for a hike.

7. Schools were all closed because the raising of the typhoon signal 3.

8. Though she is not popular, and I like her very much.

9.3 用 **before** 、 **until** 填空。

1. School is in session _____ 3:00 p.m., then we can go home.

2. You had better pack up the barbecue things _____ it starts to rain.

10. Sentences
句子

10.1 英文可以無主語嗎？

✗ Rescued <u>two starving giant pandas</u> yesterday.

✓ <u>Two starving giant pandas</u> were rescued yesterday.

昨天搶救了兩隻飢腸轆轆的大熊貓。

What's wrong?

誤句缺少主語。中文沒有主句很常見，但英文一般要有主語。漢譯英時，常用被動語態為譯文補充主語。又如：

<u>The speaker</u> made no mention of this in his report.

講者在報告裏沒提到這點。

<u>A fishing boat</u> could be seen tied up nearby.

隱約看得見一條漁船停在附近。

<u>Shouts</u> came from downstairs.

樓下傳來了叫喊聲。

There was no sound but that of <u>gunfire</u>.

除了槍聲，再沒有其他聲音。

10.2 間接賓語應放直接賓語之前嗎?

✗ I sent **my aunt it** yesterday.

✓ I sent **it** to **my aunt** yesterday.

我昨天寄了它給我姨媽。

What's wrong?

代詞 it 是及物動詞 send 的直接賓語。在直接賓語是人稱代詞的情況下,必須把間接賓語移動到直接賓語之後。

I gave **it** to **my brother**. 我把它給了我的弟弟。
He bought **it** for **his mother**. 它是他給母親買的。
Mary showed **it** to **her colleagues**.
瑪麗把它拿給她的同事們看。

Grammar Rules

如果及物動詞的雙賓語都是人稱代詞,那就更必須這麼做。例如:

Please leave **it** to **us**. 請留它給我們。
Why did you tell **it** to **them**? 你為何告訴他們這事?

> **Grammar Tips**
> 如果直接賓語是指示代詞 **this / these** 或 **that / those**,雙賓語仍可按普通語序排列。例如:
> Please give **me** **these**.
> 請給我這些。

10.3 so...that 可表示 "比較" 嗎？

✗ She speaks English <u>so well as</u> everyone admires her.

✓ She speaks English <u>so well that</u> everyone admires her.

她英語説得真好，人人都羨慕她。

What's wrong?

so...as 和 so...that 是兩個不同句型，不能混淆。前者出現於否定句，用作比較，例如：

> This novel is not <u>so interesting as</u> that one.
> 這本小説不如那本有趣。
>
> She does not speak English <u>so well as</u> Tom.
> 她英語説得不如湯姆那麼好。

後者的 so 表示程度，that 引出一個句子，表示結果，沒有比較之意。例如：

> It was <u>so noisy</u> last night <u>that</u> I could hardly fall asleep.
> 昨晚那麼吵，我幾乎睡不着。
>
> It was <u>so hot that</u> we had the air conditioner on all day.
> 天氣那麼熱，我們一整天開着空調。

10.4 表示 "一樣"，用 the same 接 like、with 嗎？

✗ He said <u>the same thing like</u> you.

✗ He said <u>the same thing with</u> you.

✓ He said <u>the same thing as</u> you.

他和你講了同樣的話。

What's wrong?

same 用作代詞或形容詞時，後接 as，形成 the same...as (sb / sth) 的結構，不後接 like 或 with。as 是關係連詞，上句其實是 He said the same thing as you did，而 like 和 with 是介詞。又如：

I had <u>the same experience as</u> you a few months ago.
我遇到了和你幾個月前同樣的經歷。

Is there another phrase that means <u>the same as</u> this?
有沒有另一個跟這短語意思一樣的？

She looks exactly <u>the same as</u> her twin sister.
她長得和她孿生妹妹一模一樣。

> **Grammar Tips**
> 用 **same** 回答對方祝願時，後接 **to**，不用 **as**。如：
> "Happy New Year!"
> "(The) <u>same to</u> you."
> "祝你新年快樂！"
> "我也祝你新年快樂。"

10.5 表示"無疑",用 no doubt 後接 if 嗎?

✗ There is **no doubt if** he will succeed in the end.

✓ There is **no doubt that** he will succeed in the end.

毫無疑問他最終會成功。

What's wrong?

no doubt 表示"無疑"、"肯定",不能後接表示疑問的連詞 if 或 whether。又如:

There is **no doubt that** Mary will pass the examination.

瑪麗肯定會考試及格。

There is **no doubt that** she will come if we invite her.

要是我們請她,她肯定會來。

> **Grammar Tips**
>
> **no doubt** 可用作副詞,這時不能再後跟 **that**,以上兩句便成為:
>
> No doubt Mary will pass the examination.
>
> No doubt she will come if we invite her.

10.6 表示 "找人修理" ，只說 repair 嗎？

✗ Where did you <u>repair</u> your car?

✓ Where did you <u>have your car repaired</u>?

你在哪裏修理汽車？

What's wrong?

汽車不會自我修理，repair 應用作 your car 的補足語，即是 "主語 + 及物動詞 + 賓語 + 賓語補足語（過去分詞）" 的句型。又如：

I <u>had</u> my shoes <u>mended</u>.
我去補了補鞋子。

She <u>had</u> herself <u>photographed</u>.
她請人替自己拍了照。

I <u>had</u> my decayed tooth <u>pulled</u> out yesterday.
我昨天拔了一顆蛀牙。

You'd better <u>have</u> your lungs <u>X-rayed</u>.
你最好對肺部做一次 X 光檢查。

10.7 表示進行的動作，賓語補足語用現在分詞嗎？

✗ I'm sorry to have <u>kept you waited</u> so long.

✓ I'm sorry to have <u>kept you waiting</u> so long.

對不起，讓你久等了。

What's wrong?

wait 是 you 的補足語，它的邏輯主語是 you，因此必須是現在分詞，表示正在進行的動作。這實際上是 "主語 + 及物動詞 + 賓語 + 賓語補足語 (現在分詞)" 的結構。又如：

I <u>saw</u> her <u>smoking</u>.
我看見她在抽煙。

She <u>heard</u> her mother <u>singing</u> in the kitchen.
她聽見她母親在廚房裏唱歌。

The teacher <u>caught</u> Tom <u>dozing off</u> in class.
老師發現湯姆上課睡着了。

Susan tried to <u>start</u> the engine <u>running</u>.
蘇珊嘗試開動引擎。

10.8 表示大概數，副詞該緊靠被修飾的數詞嗎？

✗ The journey <u>about takes</u> five hours.

✓ The journey <u>takes about</u> five hours.

路上大約要花五個小時。

What's wrong?

誤句受中文思維影響，about 的詞序不正確，應直接修飾數詞。又如：

It is <u>about</u> 9 o'clock.

現在大約 9 點鐘。

Learn More

英文有許多表示大概數的副詞或短語，它的位置總是緊靠被修飾的數詞之前或之後。例如：

She is 45 <u>or thereabouts</u>.
她約 45 歲左右。

Thirty <u>or so</u> people were invited to the wedding.
約 30 個人應邀參加婚禮。

Prices have risen by <u>roughly</u> 10%.
物價上漲了大約一成。

George earns <u>approximately</u> 40,000 dollars a year.
喬治一年大約賺四萬元。

10.9 如何用 hardly 表示強調？

✗ <u>Hardly</u> I <u>could</u> believe it.

✓ <u>Hardly</u> <u>could</u> I believe it.

我幾乎不能相信這事。

What's wrong?

hardly 置於句首表示強調，could 要移至主語之前，形成局部倒裝句。又如：

> <u>Hardly</u> <u>can</u> I hear her.
> 我幾乎聽不到她在說甚麼。

> <u>Hardly</u> a house <u>did</u> they see.
> 他們幾乎看不到一戶人家。

Grammar Rules

barely、never、not、rarely、scarcely 等否定副詞或含否定意思的副詞若置於句首，情態動詞或助動詞要移到主語之前，形成局部倒裝句。例如：

> <u>Never</u> <u>have</u> I heard of this man.
> 我從沒聽說過這個人。

> <u>Rarely</u> <u>does</u> she go there now.
> 她現在很少去那裏。

> <u>Scarcely</u> <u>had</u> he arrived when he had to leave again.
> 他剛來到就要走。

10.10 如何用 only 表示強調？

✗ <u>Only</u> by plane we <u>could</u> arrive there in time.

✓ <u>Only</u> by plane <u>could</u> we arrive there in time.

只有搭飛機我們才能及時趕到那裏。

What's wrong?

only 用於限制句子的某個成分，當 only 和被限制的成分給移到句首，情態動詞或助動詞要移至主語之前，以形成局部倒裝句。又如：

<u>Only</u> last week <u>did</u> we visit that museum.
上星期我們才參觀了那個博物館。

<u>Only</u> in China <u>can</u> you see such happy children.
只有在中國，才看得到這樣幸福的孩子。

<u>Only</u> slowly <u>do</u> you learn a foreign language.
要學會一種外語只有慢慢來。

<u>Only</u> once <u>have</u> I been to Australia.
我只去過一次澳大利亞。

10.11 表示時間、地址，"小的在前，大的在後"？

✗ He passes the square <u>daily twice</u>.

✓ He passes the square <u>twice daily</u>.

他每天經過那個廣場兩次。

What's wrong?

語序錯誤。twice 比 daily 小，應排在前面。

Grammar Rules

在英語中，無論是地點狀語、時間狀語還是頻度狀語，總是小的在前，大的在後。這與中文習慣相反。例如：

She was born <u>at 10 a.m. on July 21, 1986</u>.
Jones lives <u>in 1132 Oxford Street, London, England</u>.

如果一個句子裏同時存在地點狀語和時間狀語，那麼地點狀語在前，時間狀語在後。例如：

Mary worked hard <u>in the laboratory</u> <u>yesterday</u>.
瑪麗昨天在實驗室努力工作。
Please wait for me <u>in the park</u> <u>at 3 o'clock tomorrow afternoon</u>.
明天下午 3 點請在公園等我。

10.12 表示 "任何人"，用 anybody 後接複數動詞嗎？

✗ Please tell them I'm away if <u>anybody</u> call.

✓ Please tell them I'm away if <u>anybody</u> calls.

要是有人來電話，請告訴他我出了門。

What's wrong?

anybody 或 anyone 只能代表單數，因此動詞也必須用單數。

Is <u>anybody</u> home?
有人在家嗎？

Has <u>anybody</u> brought his or her camera?
有沒有人帶了照相機？

Learn More

everybody、everyone、somebody、someone、nobody、no one 等代詞都是單數。例如：

<u>Everybody</u> likes the new teacher.
人人都喜歡新來的老師。

<u>Someone</u> is to blame for it.
某人要對這件事承擔責任。

> **Grammar Tips**
> 就算 **anybody** 代表單數，但現代英語中，人稱代詞可用 **they (he or she)**、**them (him or her)**、**their (his or her)** 等，以避開男女性別的爭議：
> <u>Nobody</u> is reviewing their lessons.
> 誰也不在複習功課。

10.13 表示 "在一起" 的 with 詞組，會影響單複數嗎？

✗ John, <u>with his dog</u>, <u>have</u> gone hunting.

✓ John, <u>with his dog</u>, <u>has</u> gone hunting.

約翰帶着他的狗去了打獵。

What's wrong?

with 詞組就算跟在主語之後，也不是主語的組成部分，它實際上是個狀語，不影響 John 的主語地位，主動詞仍用單數形式。

Grammar Rules

如果主語是單數，就算後跟由 with、together with、along with、in addition to、besides、including 引出的短語，謂語動詞仍用單數形式。又如：

John, <u>together with</u> his mother and father, <u>is</u> spending his holidays in the Bahamas.
約翰和他父母正在巴哈馬群島度假。

The old lady, <u>along with</u> her dog, <u>takes</u> a walk in the park every day.
老太太每天都帶着狗在公園裏散步。

<u>Nobody but</u> Jack and William <u>was</u> present at the funeral.
只有傑克和威廉出席了葬禮。

This novel <u>as well as</u> his other works <u>is</u> no longer available in the bookstore.
這本小說及他的其他著作在書店裏都買不到了。

10.14 表示 "不是⋯就是⋯"，用 either...or... 時單複數
有何變化？

✗ Either they or she have to help the old man.

✓ Either they or she has to help the old man.

不是他們就是她要去幫那個老人。

What's wrong?

如果 either...or... 用作主語，謂語動詞的單複數形式取
決於 or 後面的名詞或代詞。又如：

Either I or he is wrong.
不是我錯就是他錯。

Either they or she is going to do the work.
這工作不是由他們去做就是由她去做。

Learn More

如果 neither...nor... 用作主語，謂語動詞的單複數形式
應作同樣安排。例如：

Neither Mary nor I am able to convince him.
瑪麗和我都不能說服他。

Neither the Smiths nor their daughter was at
the party.
史密斯和他們女兒都沒出席派對。

Grammar Tips
either...or... 的主謂一致越來越不嚴格。許多人常將兩
個主語合在一起用作複數。

10.15 表示"這類"，用 kind of 後跟複數名詞嗎？

✗ That <u>kind of books</u> <u>are</u> no longer popular nowadays.

✓ That <u>kind of book</u> <u>is</u> no longer popular nowadays.

這類書現在不再受歡迎。

What's wrong?

kind 是可數名詞，可以說 that kind 或 those kinds，
如 kind 用作主語，句子結構可用以下公式表示：
kind of + 可數名詞單數 / 不可數名詞 + 動詞單數形式
kinds of + 可數名詞複數 / 不可數名詞 + 動詞複數形式
比較：

This <u>kind of</u> snake <u>is</u> really dangerous.
這種蛇真的很危險。

These <u>kinds of</u> animals <u>are</u> rare now.
這幾種動物現在很稀有。

What <u>kind of</u> man <u>is</u> Jack?
傑克是哪種人？

There <u>are</u> many <u>kinds of</u> pressure cookers available on the market.
市場上有多種壓力鍋出售。

Grammar Rules

sort 的使用規則與 kind 相同。例如：

Some <u>sort</u> of compromise <u>seems</u> inevitable.
某種妥協似乎是不可避免的。

There <u>are</u> many <u>sorts of</u> cameras in this shop.
這店裏有多款照相機。

10.16 表示 "唯一"，用 the only one of，動詞是單數嗎？

✗ William is <u>the only one of</u> the club members who <u>have</u> been to Paris.

✓ William is <u>the only one of</u> the club members who <u>has</u> been to Paris.

俱樂部成員之中只有威廉一人到過巴黎。

What's wrong?

受 only 的影響，定語從句修飾的不是 club members，而是 the only one，因此從句的主動詞要用單數。

Mary is <u>one of</u> the young women in the house who smoke.

瑪麗是屋裏抽煙的年輕女子之一。

Mary is <u>the only one of</u> the young women in the house who smokes.

屋裏的年輕女子當中只有瑪麗抽煙。

Tom is <u>one of</u> my classmates who have failed the examination.

湯姆是我考試不及格的同學之一。

Tom is <u>the only one of</u> my classmates who has failed the examination.

我的同學當中只有湯姆考試不及格。

10.17 表示某類人，用 the + 形容詞，動詞是複數嗎？

✗ **The disabled is** well looked after in this community.

✓ **The disabled are** well looked after in this community.

這個社區裏殘疾人士受到很好的照顧。

What's wrong?

形容詞或分詞加定冠詞用作名詞 (如 the old 、 the young 、 the blind 、 the weak 、 the rich 、 the poor 、 the dying 、 the wounded) ，是指某種人，一般是複數，如用作主語，動詞要用複數形式。

The rich are not always happy.
有錢人不總是很快樂。

The strong always try to bully the weak in this world.
這世界總是弱肉強食。

The righteous applaud the verdict.
正直的人們為這場判決喝采。

The fittest survive in the animal kingdom.
在動物王國裏，適者生存。

10.18 表示委員會成員，用 the committee，動詞是複數嗎？

✗ <u>The committee</u> <u>is</u> arguing among itself.

✓ <u>The committee</u> <u>are</u> arguing among themselves.
 <u>委員會成員當中意見不一。</u>

What's wrong?

committee 在這裏指的是委員會成員 (committee members)，不是指這個組織，所以成員之間才可以"意見不一"，主動詞因此要用複數形式。

Grammar Rules

除 committee 外，還有 club、family、government、jury、militia、staff、team 均可指組織，也可指成員，視乎上下文而定，前者動詞用單數，後者用複數。例如：

Every <u>family</u> in the neighbourhood has a car.
這個居民小區每個家庭都有車。

My <u>family</u> are all well-educated.
我們家的人都受過良好教育。

A tennis <u>club</u> was established yesterday.
昨天成立了一個網球俱樂部。

The <u>club</u> have voted to admit 2 new members.
俱樂部會員投票接納兩個新會員。

> **Grammar Tips**
> 美式和英式英語在這方面用法不完全相同，要注意兩者的差異。

10.19 表示 "不只一人"，用 more than one，動詞是複數嗎？

✗ <u>More than one</u> <u>were</u> on the scene when the accident happened.

✓ <u>More than one</u> <u>was</u> on the scene when the accident happened.

事故發生時不只一人在現場。

What's wrong?

more than one 雖然是複數，但用作主語時，語法上仍是 one，主動詞因此要用單數形式。又如：

<u>More than one</u> <u>knows</u> the news.
不只一個人知道這個消息。

Learn More

類似結構還有 more than a、many a，主動詞都用單數形式。例如：

<u>Many a</u> woman <u>likes</u> to marry a rich man.
許多女人喜歡嫁個有錢人。

<u>More than a</u> good man <u>has been destroyed</u> by drugs.
許多好人毀於毒品。

10.20 説 "我認為不會"，I think 的否定式該如何表達？

✗ <u>I think</u> he will not accept the job.

✓ <u>I don't think</u> he will accept the job.

我認為他不會接受這份工作。

What's wrong?

誤句不符合英文習慣。如果主動詞是 think，後面的賓語從句帶否定意義，英文習慣會將否定形式放在主句。又如：

I <u>didn't think</u> you liked cooking.

我以為你不喜歡烹飪。

Learn More

含 believe、expect、imagine、suppose 等動詞的賓語從句，如帶否定意義，也作同樣處理。例如：

I <u>don't believe</u> it's going to snow tomorrow.

我認為明天不會下雪。

I <u>don't suppose</u> they'll be divorced.

我認為他們不會離婚。

She <u>didn't expect</u> he'd be so unreasonable.

她以為他不會那麼無理。

10.21 用 sure 和 certain 表示"肯定"，意思都一樣嗎？

✗ It is <u>sure</u> that Susan will win the competition.

✓ It is <u>certain</u> that Susan will win the competition.
可以肯定蘇珊會贏得比賽。

What's wrong?

sure 和 certain 是兩個意義相似的形容詞，常可以替代使用。例如：

I'm <u>sure</u> / <u>certain</u> that Mary will be late.
我敢肯定瑪麗會遲到。

Make <u>sure</u> / <u>certain</u> that all the windows are closed before you leave the room.
離開房間前要注意關好所有窗。

He's <u>sure</u> / <u>certain</u> to come tomorrow.
他明天肯定來。

但 sure 唯獨不能用於 "it is sure that + 從句" 的句型，certain 卻可以。又如：

It is <u>certain</u> that these Rolex watches are real.
這些勞力士手錶肯定是真貨。

It is <u>certain</u> that the dictionary will be published this year.
詞典今年肯定會出版。

10.22 賓語從句該用疑問句形式嗎？

✗ She asked me <u>how many</u> hours <u>did I spend</u> on studies every day?

✓ She asked me <u>how many</u> hours I spent on studies every day.

她問我每天花多少個小時學習。

What's wrong?

賓語從句不用疑問句形式，除關係代詞、關係副詞引出的部分之外，主句必須恢復陳述句語序。又如：

He asked her <u>how</u> old she was.
他問她年紀多大。

Jack told me <u>where</u> he lived.
約克告訴我他住在那裏。

Can you tell me <u>which</u> way leads to the station?
請問到車站該怎樣走？

Grammar Rules

賓語從句還包括介詞賓語從句，它的語序與動詞賓語的語序相同。例如：

The accident took place near <u>where</u> we were playing.
事故離我們玩耍處不遠發生。

This is like <u>what</u> we saw yesterday.
這很像我們昨天看到的。

10.23 the reason 之後可否不帶 why？

✗ I don't know <u>the reason</u> she looks so happy today.

✓ I don't know <u>the reason why</u> she looks so happy today.

我不知道她今天為何那麼高興。

What's wrong?

誤句缺少 why，定語從句必須含具引導作用的關係詞，否則無法與主句中的成分發生關係。又如：

The story took place at a time <u>when</u> he was young.

這故事發生於他年輕時代。

She couldn't say <u>what</u> it was that bothered her.

她說不清是甚麼令自己心煩。

I met the boatman <u>who</u> had taken me across the ferry.

我碰到那個載過我的船夫。

This is the book from <u>which</u> she quoted that paragraph?

她引用那段話就是出自這本書。

10.24 hard、necessary 可後接由 that 引出的句子嗎？

✗ <u>It is hard that</u> we have to finish the work within two hours.

✓ <u>It is hard for us to</u> finish the work within two hours.

我們要在兩小時內完成任務是很難的。

What's wrong?

在英語中，有些形容詞不後接由 that 或其他關係詞所引出的句子，採用 "It + be + 形容詞 + for sb + 動詞不定式" 的句型。又如：

<u>It is necessary for</u> you to make up your mind now.
你現在就必須決定。

<u>It is easy for</u> her to pass the test.
測驗及格對她來說很容易。

<u>It is common for</u> women to go out to work now.
婦女出外工作現在很普遍。

<u>It is convenient for</u> me to make the arrangement.
由我安排很方便。

10.25 it 後跟複數時，動詞是單數還是複數？

✗ Who broke the window? <u>It were Tom and Jack.</u>

✓ Who broke the window? <u>It was Tom and Jack.</u>

誰打破了窗？是湯姆和傑克。

What's wrong?

it 用作指示代詞，無論指的東西是單數還是複數，動詞 be 總是使用單數。又如：

Who is playing the piano?— <u>It's</u> Mary.
誰在彈鋼琴？ —— 是瑪麗。

Who is singing so loudly? — <u>It's</u> the children.
誰唱歌唱得那麼響亮？ —— 是孩子們。

Oh, <u>it's</u> you!
哦，是你呀！

<u>It's</u> the girls coming back from school.
是女孩們放學回來。

10.26 it ... be 含複數名詞時，動詞用複數嗎？

✗ <u>It are earthquakes</u> that do real damage to the buildings.

✓ <u>It is earthquakes</u> that do real damage to the buildings.

真正對建築物造成損壞的是地震。

What's wrong?

在強調句型中，無論被強調成分是單數還是複數，it be 結構總是單數，它的時態隨原句時態而定。又如：

<u>It was John and his sister</u> that helped me review my lessons.
幫我複習功課的是約翰和他妹妹。

<u>It was a scooter</u> that my father gave me as a birthday present.
我爸爸送我的生日禮物是一部滑板車。

<u>It was three foreign friends</u> who visited our school yesterday.
昨天參觀我們學校的是三個外國朋友。

<u>It is because</u> he smoked too much that he has got lung cancer.
他患肺癌因他抽煙太多。

10.27 表示 "我覺得"，可單獨用 find 嗎？

✗ I <u>find most convenient to</u> pay my bills with a credit card.

✓ I <u>find it most convenient to</u> pay my bills with a credit card.

我覺得用信用卡付賬很方便。

What's wrong?

不定式如何與句子發生關係不清楚，必須在動詞後面用先行代詞 it 作賓語才能説明它的地位。又如：

<u>We consider</u> it necessary to change our plan right away.

我們認為有必要立即改變計劃。

Grammar Rules

it 用作先行代詞還可以代替動名詞、從句等，在句中用作形式賓語，起到平衡句子的作用。(參看《英語語法速遞》15.3.1) 例如：

<u>She finds it</u> very enjoyable working with me.

她覺得跟我合作很愉快。

<u>I have made it clear</u> that I will not marry her under any circumstances.

我已明確表示，我在任何情況下都不會娶她。

10.28 轉述別人的話，yesterday 保持不變嗎？

"I finished the book <u>yesterday</u>," Susan said.
　　⟶

✗ Mary said she had finished the book <u>yesterday</u>.

✓ Mary said she had finished the book <u>the day before</u>.

瑪麗說："我昨天看完了那本書。" ⟶ 瑪麗說她前一天看完了那本書。

What's wrong?

直接引語變成間接引語時，時間狀語要作相應變化 (參見《英語語法速遞 (修訂版)》14.3)，句中的 yesterday 要變成 the day before。又如：

He said,"She is leaving for Shanghai <u>tomorrow</u>." ⟶
　　He said she was leaving for Shanghai <u>the next day</u>.

他說："她明天去上海。" ⟶ 他說她第二天去上海。

"I'm going to the cinema <u>tonight</u>," William said.
⟶

　　William said he was going to the cinema <u>that night</u>.

威廉說："我今晚要去看電影。" ⟶ 威廉說他那晚要去看電影。

10.29 轉述別人的話，時態如何一致？

She said, "I <u>moved</u> to this city last year." ⟶

✗ She said she <u>moved</u> to that city the year before.

✓ She said she <u>had moved</u> to that city the year before.

她説："我去年搬到這個城市。"⟶ 她説她前一年搬到那個城市。

What's wrong?

直接引語變為間接引語時，引語中動詞的時態須與主句動詞的時態保持一致 (參看《英語語法速遞》14.3)。誤句中的過去式要改成過去完成式。又如：

Mary said, "I'm writing a book on environmental protection." ⟶

    Mary said she <u>was writing</u> a book on environmental protection.

    瑪麗説她正在寫一本關於環境保護的書。

My mother said, "Oh, I've left my purse in the store." ⟶

    My mother said she <u>had left</u> her purse in the store.

    我媽媽説："哦，我丟了錢包在店裏。"⟶ 我媽媽説她丟了錢包在店裏。

> ### Grammar Tips
> 含絕對的時間狀語時，過去式不需要變成過去完成式。
>   She said, "I <u>moved</u> to this city in 2000." ⟶
>   She said she <u>moved</u> to that city in 2000.
>   她説："我是 2000 年搬到這城市的。"⟶ 她説她是 2000 年搬到那城市的。

10.30 轉述別人的話，仍用疑問句詞序嗎？

"Are you coming with me?" she said to me.

     $\longrightarrow$

✗ She asked me <u>was I going</u> with her?

✓ She asked me if/whether <u>I was going</u> with her.

她對我說："你跟我一起來嗎？" $\longrightarrow$ 她問我是不是跟她一起去。

What's wrong?

直接引語中的疑問句或否定疑問句，變成間接引語之後，不再是疑問句語序，也不再用問號，而用連詞 whether 或 if。又如：

"Have you been to Britain?" Tom asked Mary. $\longrightarrow$
Tom asked Mary if she <u>had been</u> to Britain.
湯姆問瑪麗："你去過英國嗎？" $\longrightarrow$ 湯姆問瑪麗有沒有去過英國。

"Your father is an engineer, isn't he?" she said to him. $\longrightarrow$
She asked him whether his father <u>was</u> an engineer.
她對他說："你爸爸是工程師，對嗎？" $\longrightarrow$ 她問他爸爸是不是工程師。

10.31 轉述別人的問句，疑問詞放哪裏？

She said to me, "How many students are there in your class?" ⟶

✗ She asked me how many students <u>were there</u> in my class?

✓ She asked me how many students <u>there were</u> in my class.

她問我："你班上有多少個學生？" ⟶ 她問我班上有多少個學生。

What's wrong?

直接引語中的特殊疑問句變成間接引語時，不再用疑問句語序，也不再用問號。但原有的疑問詞仍然前置。又如：

"How long <u>will it</u> take to get to the post office, Officer?" she asked the policeman. ⟶

She asked the policeman how long <u>it would</u> take to get to the post office.

她問警察："到郵局要花多長時間，長官？" ⟶ 她問警察到郵局要花多長時間。

She asked me, "Whose bike <u>did you use</u> <u>yesterday</u>?" ⟶

She asked me whose bike I <u>had used</u> <u>the day</u> <u>before</u>.

她問我："你昨天用誰的自行車？" ⟶ 她問我昨天用誰的自行車。

Practice 練習 10

10.1 改正錯誤。

1. Living standards in China have raised greatly in the past few years.
    _____

2. I bought a birthday present and sent her it.
    _____

3. Where did you cut your hair?
    _____

4. Buying clothes are often a time-consuming thing.
    _____

5. Ten minutes are all I can spare to discuss the matter with you.
    _____

6. Mary is the only one of my classmates who have learned shorthand.
    _____

7. Neither Jack nor his parents knows how to use the computer.
    _____

8. Rarely we see such stamps now.
    _____

9. She used to his bad temper.
    _____

10. It were John and William who rescued the drowning girl.

_____

11. I think he will not come tomorrow.

_____

12. She lives in Washington, U.S.A. in 300 E Street.

_____

10.2 用以下詞彙重組句子。

1. quietly in line stand.

_____

2. to put my card octopus on more money I have

_____

3. I could so hungry I'm eat a horse

_____

4. not quiet not continue if you are will we

_____

5. two boys those saw us except leave nobody

_____

6. a cute and matching water a bottle keychain along with a notebook bought pens and I

_____

7. the only always has some who saves my little brother one of us is his money to spare and

_____

8. the neighbourhood for everyone looks out everyone in else

   _____

9. even more he loved life his parents than itself

   _____

10. piece belongs to that I the puzzle found missing the

    _____

11. it is kill that people it is not buildings earthquakes that kill people

    _____

12. going it looks a to be like it's day nice to be

    _____

13. long how Bart John asked to take the test going was

    _____

11. Vocabulary
詞彙

11.1 表示 "習慣於" 用 used to 嗎？

✗ Soon after, he <u>used to</u> the way of life in the neighbourhood.

✓ Soon after, he <u>got used to</u> the way of life in the neighbourhood.

不多久他就習慣了那個居民小區的生活模式。

What's wrong?

used 和 get used/be used 在含義和詞性兩方面都完全不同。used 是情態動詞，表示過去慣常的事實或狀態，後接不定式； get used / be used 的 used 是形容詞，表示 "習慣於"，與 to 連用，後接名詞或動名詞。比較：

I <u>used to</u> live with my parents.
我過去一直跟父母住在一起。

I <u>am used to</u> living with my parents.
我習慣跟父母住在一起。

Susan <u>used to</u> like wine.
蘇珊過去愛喝酒。

Susan <u>has got used to</u> Chinese food.
蘇珊已習慣吃中菜。

> **Grammar Tips**
> **used** 藉 **did** 構成否定句及疑問句。例如：
> <u>Did</u> you <u>use to</u> live in Washington?
> 你過去一直住在華盛頓嗎？
> I <u>didn't use to</u> swim when I was young.
> 我年輕時不常游泳。

11.2 表示 "為某物花多少錢" cost 可與 on 連用嗎？

✗ I cost five dollars on this book.
✓ I spent five dollars on this book.
  我花了五塊錢買這本書。

What's wrong?

cost 和 spend 雖然都解作 "花費"，但兩者含義有差異。cost 是 "某物使某人花費多少錢"，spend 則是 "某人為某物花費多少錢"。比較：

The colour —— TV set cost me 200 dollars.
這部彩色電視機花了我 200 美元。

I spent 200 dollars on the colour —— TV set.
我花了 200 美元買這部彩色電視機。

The new hospital cost the village 100,000 yuan.
蓋這座新醫院花去村裏 10 萬元。

The village spent 100,000 yuan building the new hospital.
村裏花去 10 萬元蓋這座新醫院。

11.3 表示 "提高價錢" 用 rise 嗎？

✗ The store <u>rose</u> the retail price of chocolate again.

✓ The store <u>raised</u> the retail price of chocolate again.

商店又提高了巧克力的零售價。

What's wrong?

rise 是不及物動詞 ，不可跟直接賓語，只可表示 "價格上升" ，不可說 "提高價格" ，後者要用及物動詞 raise 。比較：

The price of pork <u>has risen</u> by 20%. 豬肉價錢漲了兩成。

The butcher <u>has raised</u> the price of pork by 20%. 肉商將豬肉價錢提高了兩成。

Comparison

rise 和 raise 還可表示數量、水平、標準、薪金等有所提高，但用法與上述規則相同。比較兩組例句：

Industrial output <u>rose</u> by 10% in January. 一月份工業產量增加 10%。

The factory <u>was</u> renovated to <u>raise</u> the output. 工廠翻新過以提高產量。

The wages <u>have risen</u> by 20% this year. 今年工資增長了 20%。

The boss <u>raised</u> the wages of his workers by 20%. 老闆將他工人的工資提高了 20%。

11.4 表示 "長幼關係" 用 old 嗎？

✗ My <u>older</u> brother is studying in Britain.

✓ My <u>elder</u> brother is studying in Britain.

我哥哥在英國讀書。

What's wrong?

兄弟姐妹之間的長幼關係不可用 old 表示，而要用 elder 及 eldest。

He is <u>the eldest</u> of the three brothers.
他是三兄弟中的老大。

William is my <u>elder</u> / <u>eldest</u> brother.
威廉是我哥哥 / 大哥。

Mary is his <u>elder</u> / <u>eldest</u> sister.
瑪麗是他姐姐 / 大姐。

但可以説 one's <u>eldest</u> son / daughter（某人的長子 / 長女）。

Learn More

old 用於比較年齡。例如：

He is the <u>oldest</u> of the three men.
他是三人之中年紀最大的。

My elder sister is two years <u>older</u> than I.
我姐姐比我大兩歲。

11.5 指"人的高度"用 high 嗎？

✗ This tree must be 20 metres <u>high</u>.

✓ This tree must be 20 metres <u>tall</u>.

這樹一定有 20 米高。

What's wrong?

樹高不説 high，而説 tall。high 和 tall 都是"高"的意思，但修飾對象不同。high 指從底到頂的距離或離地面的高度。例如：

Mount Qomolangma is <u>the highest</u> mount in the world.
珠穆朗瑪峰是世界上的最高峰。

The plane was 8,000 metres <u>high</u> when it exploded.
飛機爆炸時正處於 8,000 米高空。

How <u>high</u> is the wall?
這牆有多高？

tall 用於表示人的身高、樹幹等事物，例如：

George is <u>the tallest</u> in our class.
佐治是我們班上個子最高的。

How <u>tall</u> do you think the flagpole is?
你認為這旗杆有多高？

That <u>tall</u> oak collapsed in the thunderstorm.
那棵高大的橡樹在雷暴中倒下來。

11.6 表示"去過"，用 has / have gone to 嗎？

✗ My uncle <u>has gone to</u> London twice.

✓ My uncle <u>has been to</u> London twice.

我叔叔去過兩次倫敦。

What's wrong?

從中文角度來看，"去過"和"去了"是兩種不同概念。"去過"表示"以前去了，現在已回來，成了一種經歷"；"去了"表示"現在還沒有回來"。英語中存在同樣差異，前者用 have been to，後者用 have gone to 表達。比較下列兩組例句：

Jane <u>has gone to</u> New York.
珍去了紐約。

Jane <u>has never been to</u> New York.
珍從來沒去過紐約。

She <u>has gone to</u> the cinema.
她去看了部電影。

She <u>has been to</u> the cinema twice this week.
她這個星期已看過兩次電影。

11.7 表示 "算不上"，用 not 或 no？

✗ His sister is <u>no doctor</u>.

✓ His sister is <u>not a doctor</u>.

他姐姐不是醫生。

What's wrong?

no 和 not 在這裏是兩個完全不同的概念，詞性也不同。not 是副詞，用於對句子的否定；no 是形容詞，意思是 "算不上"。比較：

My brother is <u>not</u> a teacher. 我弟弟不是老師。
My brother is <u>no</u> teacher. 我弟弟算不上是老師。
She is <u>not</u> a physicist. 她不是物理學家。
She is <u>no</u> physicist. 她算不上是物理學家。

> **Grammar Tips**
>
> 副詞 **no** 被用以表示否定回答，置於答句之首，常與 **not** 一起使用，例如：
>
> Is this a space shuttle? <u>No</u>, it is <u>not</u> a space shuttle.
> 這是太空穿梭機嗎？不，這不是太空穿梭機。
>
> 注意，不要讓這種語言現象引起兩者使用上的混淆。

11.8 不用 fat 形容肥胖，可用甚麼字？

✗ You are looking a bit <u>fat</u>.

✓ You are looking a bit <u>overweight</u>.

你看上去有點胖。

What's wrong?

書面語中或在別人背後，有人會用 fat 形容人胖。

> She will surely grow <u>fat</u> if she keeps on eating so much chocolate.
> 要是她繼續吃那麼多巧克力，她肯定會長胖。
>
> My aunt is a <u>fat</u> woman. 我姨媽是個胖女人。

但是，當着別人的面説他 fat，會引起反感，甚至得罪別人，應該避免使用 fat。overweight 比 fat 較為中性，有胖的意思，也表示不大健康。例如：

> You're a little <u>overweight</u>. Are you going on a diet?
> 你有點發福。你打算節食嗎？
>
> I'm a bit <u>overweight</u>. 我體重有點超過正常。

用 large 形容胖也不易惹人反感。

> Your mother is a rather <u>large</u> woman.
> 你媽媽相當胖。

> **Grammar Tips**
> fat 的反義詞是 **thin**。用 **thin**，使人聯想起"皮黃骨瘦"、"皮包骨"，宜用 **slim**。例如：
> His mother looks rather <u>thin</u> after illness.
> 他媽媽生病後看上去很瘦。
> You are getting <u>slimmer</u>, Mary. 瑪麗，你越來越苗條了。

Practice 練習 11

11.1 改正錯誤。

1. He used to travelling to work by train.

    _____

2. John cost ten thousand dollars on this new computer.

    _____

3. The supermarket rose the price of fresh vegetables.

    _____

4. His older son is three years older than I.

    _____

5. The ceiling of this building is tall.

    _____

6. Jack has gone to Shanghai twice.

    _____

7. My sister is no lawyer.

    _____

8. You are getting a bit fat, aren't you?

    _____

11.2 選詞填空。

1. borrow / loan

    I forgot to bring my math book. Can I _____ yours?

    Could you _____ me $10 so I have enough to buy a drink?

2. economical / economy

The _____ of Hong Kong is so good, the Government has a surplus of money.

It is _____ to compare prices so you get the most for your money.

3. wish / hope

I _____ I could be invisible.

I _____ you will come to my party this weekend.

4. bored / boring

This is the most _____ game in the world.

Let's do something. I'm _____.

Only _____ people get _____.

5. tell / ask

Could you _____ me what the password is?

Since we are lost, let's _____ someone to help us.

6. give away / take away

Our cat had five kittens. We are keeping one so we have four to _____.

We can eat here or get our food to _____.

7. close / closed

We are 1 minute too late. The shop is _____.

_____ the cage door so the bird doesn't fly out.

8. million / millions

If you had one _____ dollars, what would you spend it on?

Even though Hong Kong is small in land area, _____ of people live here.

9. outlook / appearance

Pat cares about her _____ and always tries to look her best.

The weather _____ for tomorrow is perfect for our hike in the country park.

10. much / many

How _____ times do I have to tell you to turn down the volume?

How _____ money do we need to bring on our trip?

11. fewer / less

We take our own bags to the market and so we use _____ plastic bags.

It takes _____ time to walk up the stairs than to wait for the lift–it is so slow.

12. staff / staffs

All of the office _____ got a pay raise.

His uncle carves wooden _____ and sells them to hikers.

Answers
答案

Practice 練習 1

1.1

1. *Physics is an interesting subject.*
2. *A cat has nine lives.*
3. *The book is covered with dust.*
4. *I have lots of schoolwork to do this evening.*
5. *The lower branches of the tree almost touch the ground.*
6. *Twelve police / policemen are working on that case.*
7. *Two Dutchmen sailed to Japan this morning.*
8. *This pair of shoes is not on sale.*

1.2

1. *You need to tidy up your hair.*
2. *The government is recruiting responsible young adults to become policemen and women.*
3. *That woman at the information desk can answer all of our questions.*
4. *To drink, all I want is a glass of water.*
5. *For our project we are doing some research on how plants suck water up into their leaves.*
6. *The school secretary's briefcase was found under a bench.*
7. *I don't know what's wrong. I feel tired all the time.*
8. *That bunch of bananas in the bowl looks very pretty.*
9. *Hundreds of containers hold all kinds of cargo at the Kwai Chung terminal.*
10. *There are three different kinds of bamboo in the garden.*

Practice 練習 2

2.1

1. My mother bought an electric iron yesterday.
2. This table is made of oak.
3. Jack left school at the age of 17.
4. Some people go to church and some don't.
5. Man has taken its first step into space.
6. If winter comes, can spring be far behind?
7. The wounded were immediately taken to a hospital nearby.
8. My brother showed me how to fly a kite.

2.2

1. We might go to <u>the</u> Philippines or maybe to Ø Australia.
2. Can you see <u>the</u> Pacific Ocean from Ø Ocean Park?
3. I plan to go to <u>a</u> university in Hong Kong when I leave Ø school.
4. <u>An</u> umbrella is essential in <u>the</u> rainy season.
5. Ø Moonlight is Ø sunlight reflected from <u>the</u> surface of <u>the</u> moon.
6. I had Ø soup and a sandwich for Ø lunch and Ø fruit for Ø dessert.
7. <u>A</u> bird in <u>the</u> hand is worth two in <u>the</u> bush.
8. I don't know how old my grandfather is. He was born in <u>the</u> 1950s.
9. My specialty in track and field events is <u>the</u> long jump.
10. The school put up a net so now we can play Ø volleyball or Ø badminton.

3.1

1. *Is there anybody who would like to go swimming with me?*
2. *The baby cried for its mother.*
3. *When John went to town, he bought some chocolate for his brother and himself.*
4. *Those who are interested in these magazines may borrow them.*
5. *It's impossible for Jack and me to finish our task before dark.*
6. *This umbrella is mine; that one is hers.*
7. *The ink is used up. I have to buy a new bottle.*
8. *None of us speaks Russian very well.*

3.2

Across / Down	a	b	c	d	e	f	g	h	i	j	k	l	m	n	o	p	q
1							w			t	h	e	i	r	s		
2						w	h	i	c	h		t			h	i	m
3							o			e			m	e			
4							m			m	i	n	e				
5										s							
6			p		n	e	i	t	h	e	r						
7			a		o					l							
8			i		n					v							
9	h	e	r	s	e	l	f			e							
10										s							

横

1 j This desk does not belong to our class so it must be <u>theirs</u>.

2 f I can't decide <u>which</u> I like better.

2 o Albert said please return the book to <u>him</u>, when you have finished with it.

3 n The principal spoke to my friend about <u>me</u>.

4 j You can't have it, it's <u>mine</u>!

6 e <u>Neither</u> Ed nor Jack are to blame. They both say Paul did it.

9 a She said she would do it <u>herself</u>.

直

c 6 These trousers are too short. Do you have another <u>pair</u>?

e 6 <u>None</u> of these web sites has trustworthy information.

g 1 You saw Ms Wong holding hands with <u>whom</u>?

j 1 Their teacher offered to help but the students said they could do it <u>themselves</u>.

m 1 <u>It</u> doesn't take long to do.

o 1 <u>She</u> is the girl I've been looking for.

Practice 練習 4

4.1

1. We have six fifty-minute classes every day.

2. 81 divided by 9 makes 9.

3. Many important battles took place during World War II.

4. My mother bought some two-dollar-a-kilo fish.

5. More than two hundred students attended the lecture.

6. She bought two dozen eggs in the supermarket.

7. The twelve-year-old girl is my sister.

8. The pagoda must be 50 metres tall.

4.2

1. We live on the *eighth* floor.

2. How many *times* do I have to tell you–turn off the lights when you leave the room!

3. George won the race in the 11-13 year *old* category.

4. How *much* money do you need to save to buy that computer?

5. The population of Hong Kong has grown to over seven *million* people.

6. Take these tablets twice *a day* for one week.

7. Add 1 cup of water and heat to 110 *degrees*.

8. Look at all those birds! There must be *dozens and dozens* of them.

9. There are 8 different *titles* in the Harry Potter series. Book two is my favourite.

4.3

1. If this is August, last month was *July*.

2. It's now November. In three months it will be *February*.

3. I was born in 2003. My elder brother is four years older than me. He was born in *1999*.

Practice 練習 5

5.1

A

1. How dare you talk to me like that?
2. Please pass the salt to me.
3. Written in 1939, the song is still very popular today.
4. My father asked me to study harder so that I could make greater progress.
5. On my way to work, I stopped to mail a letter.
6. Tom has been to the library twice today.
7. Walking down the street, I saw a bookstore.
8. When he was 6, his family left for Hong Kong.

B

1. He has just come back.
2. We'll stay at home if it rains tomorrow.
3. Our teacher told us that a good way to improve listening ability was to watch television.
4. When Columbus discovered America, he thought he had arrived in India.
5. Having discussed it with others, the boss accepted my proposal.
6. If the roads are not improved soon, driving in this area will become impossible.
7. If Susan had finished her thesis a little sooner, she would have gained her MA degree this summer.
8. He suggested that I (should) apply to Oxford University.

5.2

1. The traffic accident <u>happened</u> just as I crossed the street.
2. There <u>has to be</u> at least six numbers or letters in the password.
3. We have no choice. We <u>must</u> go with mother.
4. Wait until the water <u>boils</u> before pouring it into the thermos.
5. We stopped to <u>talk</u> to each other at the corner.
6. This note from the school needs <u>to be signed</u> by your parents and then returned to your teacher.
7. My baby sister <u>was born</u> in June last year.
8. John and Andy, but not Paul, <u>play</u> basketball each day after school.
9. I <u>didn't believe</u> the time could go so fast.
10. We would have been there by now if you <u>had not lost</u> the map.
11. We urged the boy <u>not to touch</u> the dead bird.

Practice 練習 6

6.1

1. The river is nearly 100 metres wide.
2. My sister's new bike costs more than Mary's.
3. She is the taller of the twin sisters.
4. Tom seems to be a worse-informed person than Jane.
5. My sister is three years older than I.
6. My computer is much inferior to yours.

7. The speech was so boring that we didn't want to listen any more.

8. The more they talked, the more encouraged they felt.

6.2

✓ There are the toilets. On the right is the women's. On the left is the men's.

✓ My very tall cousin is actually younger than me.

✓ My dog is better trained than your dog.

✓ Ask the librarian. She is the best-informed person in the whole school.

✓ We have tickets for front row seats. I'm so excited!

✓ Comparing Hong Kong, Guangzhou and Shanghai, Guangzhou has the smallest population.

✓ That computer is the least expensive.

✓ Hey! Why does Jack have a bigger piece of cake than I have?

✓ Let sleeping dogs lie.

✓ You would do well to get more exercise and fresh air.

Practice 練習 7

7.1

1. John loves Mary very much.

2. They can hardly speak English.

3. This skirt is specially designed for you.

4. The flowers in the garden are so beautiful.

5. How ever did he manage to find the lost wallet?

6. *Three hours later, they returned safe and sound.*

7. *The cave is nearly 100 metres deep.*

8. *He loves music and she does too.*

7.2

1. *I barely recognized him.*

2. *If you're not going, then I am not going either.*

3. *Do I have to? This practice is just so boring.*

4. *Are you bored? Playing a video game would be so much more interesting, right?*

5. *Wash your hands before you do anything, especially if you've been outside playing.*

6. *Put the ladder against the way and later we can climb up and clean the windows.*

7. *I haven't seen my grandmother for some time.*

8. *Here is a menu. You can order whatever you want.*

9. *Listen! I just now heard a bird singing. / Listen! I heard a bird singing just now.*

10. *He speaks English very well and works as a translator.*

Practice 練習 8

8.1

1. *Look! There are two monkeys in the trees.*

2. *When you move to a new place, it takes a lot of getting used to.*

3. *The new theatre was inaugurated on the afternoon of May 23, 2001.*

4. She participated in and learned much from the seminar.

5. I'll never forget the day on which I joined the army.

6. It was liver cancer that his grandfather died of.

7. It's easy to make friends with people like him.

8. Finally we saw a house among the trees.

8.2

I want you to meet me <u>at</u> noon, <u>on</u> / <u>at</u> the corner of Nathan Road and Jordan Road. Get <u>on</u> bus number 2 <u>at</u> the Star Ferry Pier terminus and get off after 6 stops. I suggest first we go <u>in</u> the big department store <u>on</u> / <u>at</u> the corner and look <u>at</u> the display <u>of</u> Chinese arts and handicrafts <u>on</u> the 4th floor.

8.3

1. Our school has no sports ground <u>like</u> theirs.

2. My dog understands my moods <u>as</u> if he can read my mind.

3. This bed is so comfortable, it is <u>like</u> sleeping on a cloud.

4. Treat others <u>as</u> you would like them to treat you.

5. To get the job done we need to work together <u>as</u> a team.

8.4

1. I'm trying to find a small key <u>among</u> all the junk in my desk drawer.

2. The coin fell <u>between</u> the two cushions on the couch.

8.5

1. The atmosphere <u>above</u> the earth's surface is about 1,000 km thick.

2. *If you keep eating like that you are going to weigh <u>over</u> 100 kg!*

Practice 練習 **9**

9.1

1. *While she was in college, she learned English as well as French.*
2. *Because he was ill, he did not go to school yesterday.*
3. *Though he worked hard, the boss fired him.*
4. *Tom behaved so badly at the party that nobody liked him.*
5. *The rain did not stop until noon.*
6. *You may come either by bike or on foot.*
7. *He studied well this term, so he passed the exam easily.*
8. *Despite the fact that it was raining, we worked three hours in the field.*

9.2

1. *I like all kinds of ball games, for example soccer and volleyball.*
2. *Because my watch stopped, I was late.*
3. *You left your bag unattended so it was stolen.*
4. *Pat did not study at all yet she still scored well on the test.*
5. *Because I watched a scary movie, I could not go to sleep.*
6. *We had to choose between either shopping, watching a movie or going for a hike. / We had to choose between shopping or watching a movie or going for a hike.*

7. Schools were all closed because of the raising of the typhoon signal 3. / Because of the raising of the typhoon signal 3, all schools were closed.

8. Though she is not popular, I like her very much.

9.3

1 School is in session until 3:00 p.m., then we can go home.

2. You had better pack up the barbecue things before it starts to rain.

Practice 練習 10

10.1

1. Living standards in China have risen greatly in the past few years.

2. I bought a birthday present and sent it to her.

3. Where did you have your hair cut?

4. Buying clothes is often a time-consuming thing.

5. Ten minutes is all I can spare to discuss the matter with you.

6. Mary is the only one of my classmates who has learned shorthand.

7. Neither Jack nor his parents know how to use the computer.

8. Rarely do we see such stamps now.

9. She is used to his bad temper.

10. It was John and William who rescued the drowning girl.

11. I don't think he will come tomorrow.

12. She lives in 300 E Street, Washington, U.S.A.

10.2

1. Stand in line quietly. / Quietly stand in line.
2. I have to put more money on my octopus card.
3. I'm so hungry I could eat a horse.
4. If you are not quiet we will not continue.
5. Nobody saw us leave except those two boys.
6. Along with pens and a notebook, I bought a cute keychain and a matching water bottle. / I bought pens and a notebook along with a cute water bottle and a matching keychain.
7. My little brother is the only one of us who saves his money and always has some to spare. / The only one of us who saves his money and always has some to spare is my little brother.
8. Everyone in the neighbourhood looks out for everyone else.
9. He loved his parents even more than life itself.
10. I found the missing piece that belongs to the puzzle.
11. It is not earthquakes that kill people it is buildings that kill people.
12. It looks like it's going to be a nice day.
13. John asked Bart how long the test was going to take. / Bart asked John how long the test was going to take.

Practice 練習 **11**

11.1

1. He has got used to travelling to work by train.
2. John spent ten thousand dollars on this new computer.
3. The supermarket raised the price of fresh vegetables.
4. His elder son is three years older than I.
5. The ceiling of this building is high.
6. Jack has been to Shanghai twice.
7. My sister is not a lawyer.
8. You are getting a bit overweight, aren't you?

11.2

1. I forgot to bring my math book. Can I <u>borrow</u> yours?

   Could you <u>loan</u> me $10 so I have enough to buy a drink?

2. The <u>economy</u> of Hong Kong is so good, the Government has a surplus of money.

   It is <u>economical</u> to compare prices so you get the most for your money.

3. I <u>wish</u> I could be invisible.

   I <u>hope</u> you will come to my party this weekend.

4. This is the most <u>boring</u> game in the world.

   Let's do something. I'm <u>bored</u>.

   Only <u>boring</u> people get <u>bored</u>.

5. Could you <u>tell</u> me what the password is?

   Since we are lost, let's <u>ask</u> someone to help us.

6. Our cat had five kittens. We are keeping one so we have four to <u>give away</u>.

We can eat here or get our food to <u>take away</u>.

7. *We are 1 minute too late. The shop is <u>closed</u>.*

   <u>Close</u> the cage door so the bird doesn't fly out.

8. *If you had one <u>million</u> dollars, what would you spend it on?*

   Even though Hong Kong is small in land area, <u>millions</u> of people live here.

9. *Pat cares about her <u>appearance</u> and always tries to look her best.*

   The weather <u>outlook</u> for tomorrow is perfect for our hike in the country park.

10. *How <u>many</u> times do I have to tell you to turn down the volume?*

    How <u>much</u> money do we need to bring on our trip?

11. *We take our own bags to the market and so we use <u>fewer</u> plastic bags.*

    It takes <u>less</u> time to walk up the stairs than to wait for the lift–it is so slow.

12. *All of the office <u>staff</u> got a pay raise.*

    His uncle carves wooden <u>staffs</u> and sells them to hikers.